LOVE'S GAMBLE

When Sarah Gannon's papa gambles away the family home, she is forced to open a herbalist's shop to survive. The Duke of Whitewell, in gratitude for Sarah's visits and medicines, leaves her a generous legacy upon his death. However, the new Duke suspects the worst of their innocent relationship, and Sarah is scathing in return. With such rancour between them, she never suspects why winning back Tewit Manor hasn't made her happy. When will she realise that home is where the heart is?

Books by Louise Armstrong
in the Linford Romance Library:

HOLD ON TO PARADISE
JAPANESE MAGIC
A PICTURE OF HAPPINESS
THE PRICE OF HAPPINESS
CONCRETE PROPOSAL
PATTERN OF LOVE
KINGFISHER DAYS
MASTER OF DIPLOMACY
HER GUARDIAN ANGEL

LOUISE ARMSTRONG

LOVE'S GAMBLE

Complete and Unabridged

LINFORD
Leicester

First published in Great Britain in 2006

First Linford Edition
published 2006

British Library CIP Data

Armstrong, Louise
    Love's gamble.—Large print ed.—
Linford romance library
    1. Love stories
    2. Large type books
    I. Title
    823.9'14 [F]

    ISBN 1–84617–561–5

Published by
F. A. Thorpe (Publishing)
Anstey, Leicestershire

Set by Words & Graphics Ltd.
Anstey, Leicestershire
Printed and bound in Great Britain by
T. J. International Ltd., Padstow, Cornwall

This book is printed on acid-free paper

1

The great elms that sheltered the half-timbered buildings of Tewit Manor were a glorious riot of autumn colour and a vast blue sky arched over the delightfully-leaded and gabled roof, while white doves cooed in the stable yard. Unfortunately, the inside of the house was not so tranquil. The morning-room, with its studded and worked plaster ceiling, was charmingly furnished and immaculately kept, but an emotional storm was raging between two beautiful sisters. The oldest stamped her foot and spoke out with great passion.

'I'll die if I can't go to London!'

The youngest sister, Sarah, tried her best to stay calm.

'Grace, I'm not trying to argue with you. I'm just surprised. I don't understand why you want to stay with

1

Aunt Octavia, or how you made her acquaintance.'

Grace's dark eyes were bright with emotion.

'It's none of your business! Papa says I can go.'

'Sweetheart, no-one is trying to stop you! It's just . . . Aunt Octavia . . . '

'Aunt Octavia what?' Grace demanded. 'You don't even know her!'

Sarah tried to grasp an elusive but unpleasant memory — a large dark woman with a large dark voice and a neighing laugh; her easy-going father scowling and staying out of the house from morning to night; her sweet-tempered mother weeping, terrifying in itself. Sarah had never seen her mother cry before and the servants kept quarrelling. The usually sunny ambience of Tewit Manor had changed into a poisonous fog. Young as she was, the visit had made a strong impression on her, yet her oldest sister seemed to remember nothing.

'Grace, we hardly know her. How did

the idea of this visit come about?'

'She wrote to me.'

Grace fished in her reticule for a sheet of paper that was crossed and recrossed with black spiky writing.

'Mrs Yates suggested that she ask me to stay because you and Julia are so hopelessly countrified. I will benefit so much more from a winter in London.'

'But you don't like Mrs Yates.'

'What does that matter? I'm going to stay with Aunt Octavia.'

Sarah felt dimly that it mattered a great deal, but long experience told her that it was of no use to argue with Grace when her heart was set upon a course of action. Her sister was shouting now.

'This is Aunt Octavia we're talking about, our mother's brother's widow! You're just jealous because you'll have to stay in this mouldy, old hole all winter, you and Julia.'

Grace waved a dismissive hand around the wood-panelled room, scorning the lovely, polished furniture, and the curtains that had been so pretty when Mother was a bride.

'I want to go to London. I want to meet the Prince Regent. I want to stay in a nice new house, with new furniture and soft beds and no draughts. I want to go shopping in the morning and to the theatre in the evening. I want to drive out in a barouche landau . . . '

Sarah watched helplessly as Grace rushed across the room, wrenched open the latch, whisked out and slammed the heavy oak door behind her. She was still staring at the door when it opened again and she tensed, expecting Grace to return, but their middle sister, Julia, was smiling at her from the doorway.

'Oh, Julia!' Sarah said imploringly.

Julia laughed out loud as she came into the room with a waft of cold air and the smell of gardens. She took hold of Sarah's hand, and the touch was a comfort.

'Grace's mysterious letter, I'll warrant,' Julia said gently. 'Come and sit on the sofa beside me. We'll have tea, and you shall tell me all about it.'

Julia lifted the silver teapot and clinked busily among the ivy-patterned tea service. Sarah sat obediently on the sofa and felt a wave of love for this other sister of hers. She'd always admired Julia's blonde hair, so much nicer than her own brown locks. Julia looked delicate and elegant, but she was the most vibrant human being that Sarah had ever met. Her blue eyes sparkled now as she spoke.

'Tell Julia!'

Sarah took a sip of the tea. It was hot, fragrant and refreshing.

'Nobody makes tea like you do, Julia.'

Her sister laughed again.

'And nobody creates storms like Grace does. Never was a child more misnamed than our big sister. Tell me what happened.'

Julia then said nothing until she was sure Sarah had finished. Then she regarded her with eyes that were blue as spring gentians.

'It might be good for her to go to London.'

'Perhaps,' Sarah said doubtfully, thinking of shops, assemblies and young men all ready to flirt. 'Julia, what do you know of Aunt Octavia?'

'Nothing wonderful but this visit could be the making of Grace. She's like a plant in the wrong soil. She doesn't thrive in the country. She might be happy in London.'

A heavy sigh behind them made both sisters start.

'Ah, Miss Grace is one of them who can't be happy unless she's enjoying herself. I've often marked it.'

Julia recovered first. She smiled at the housekeeper.

'Hello, Martha. I'm afraid we haven't finished tea yet.'

'You've no time for tea, Miss Julia. The pigs have got out of the orchard and Harry Starkie says he's too laid up with rheumatics to go after them.'

Dinner that night was taken over by the topic of London. Grace's dark eyes glowed and she leaned forward across the table and spoke with a happy animation that Sarah had rarely seen in her. Their father soon tired of the subject. His eyes sparkled as he prepared to tease his daughter.

'You'll have me selling up the house now and us all moving to London on the next stagecoach, so you will,' he said to Grace.

Grace sat up straight and her hand flew to her chest.

'You're teasing me, Papa! I know you'd never move.'

'And if I did, I'd go back to Ireland. But this is my home now, and when I leave, they'll carry me out in a box, see if they don't.'

Grace was not to be distracted.

'Yes, but, Papa, everyone is so smart in London. I must have some more clothes.'

'You have the same allowance as your sisters now. Why should I be giving more to you? There's no fairness in that.'

'It doesn't matter what they look like, buried in the country! They were out chasing pigs this morning. I need to look like a lady.'

For a moment, Patrick Gannon frowned, but then he recovered his good humour and roared with laughter.

'By, you remind me of your grandmother! Your mother's mother that was. Terrible that woman was when she took an idea to her head, and you're the very spit of her. Aye, they don't make them like that any more. Swore she'd never speak to your mother again if she married me and she stuck to it. Not even when Elanora had her babies, not a word passed your grandmother's lips to her own daughter. Grand lady she was, and let me tell you, Miss Grace, if your grandmother was still alive, it's no invitations to London you'd be getting from Aunt Octavia. Not a one of that family dared speak to your mother until the old lady was gone.'

Old history held no interest for Grace.

'But, Papa. I have been invited and I must have more clothes. Do you want your daughter to look a fool at the grand parties Aunt Octavia will take me to?'

Patrick showed every sign of growling at his younger daughter, but Julia rushed in to make peace.

'Grace will be out in Society more than Sarah or myself, it's true. Grace, you shall have my apple-blossom muslin to take with you. The maid will alter it to fit.'

Sarah reflected on her winter wardrobe. Her pelisse from the year before could be turned and made to do another season.

'You can take my new green pelisse.'

Grace was unmoved by her sister's gallant sacrifices.

'Altered country garments!' she cried passionately. 'I want to wear silk and fine satin!'

Patrick had had more than enough of the subject of clothes. He threw his napkin on the table and rose to his feet in a temper.

'You'll be warm and you'll be dry! What more could you want?'

Julia was the only one who dared reply.

'We have to look pretty, Papa, or no-one will want to marry us!'

Blue eyes clashed with blue, until their father softened.

'Marriage, is it? You're all too young for marrying yet. What'll your old papa do without you if you all go off and marry? But I'll not have this talk of you giving up your own pretties, my Julia. Those pigs are a dratted nuisance and Harry Starkie is beyond the management of them. Let's have them at the market and you girls shall keep the spoils.'

Restored to good humour by his clever plan, he went off to the library to play a game of billiards with the butler. Grace was ecstatic.

'I've never been so happy!' she declared, and then a calculating expression appeared in her eyes. 'How much is a pig worth?'

The autumn weather stayed mostly fine and the atmosphere at Tewit Manor continued sunny over the winter. They soon got used to being without Grace, and country life continued its tranquil round. Julia loved the outdoor life. The land and the livestock were her domain, and the herb garden her greatest joy.

Sarah was happiest inside the beautiful, old house. She would hum to herself as she moved lightly from room to lovely room, supervising the myriad tasks that went into running a smooth home throughout the winter. Whenever she had a few spare moments, she would slip to her still-room and potter contentedly, turning Julia's herbs into salves and useful tisanes, then experimenting for sheer pleasure with beauty lotions and potions.

She was there towards the end of a grey February day, when Julia came to find her.

'A letter from Grace. Come and have tea with me and we'll read it together.'

11

Sarah stopped stirring a bowl full of rose-scented soap.

'Is it that time already? I didn't even hear the mail.'

Julia laughed as she tucked her arm under Sarah's and pulled her away.

'You never hear anything once you get mixing your potions. It smells like summer in here.'

They decided to have tea in the library and Martha carried in the tray. Julia shook out a heavy sheet of cream parchment, covered on both sides with large, schoolgirl letters in blue ink.

'I'll read you Grace's letter first. We'll save the seed catalogues for later. She starts by saying thank you for our letters. She says she's been too busy to write to us. Let's see. She has been shopping every day, likes driving in Aunt Octavia's carriage, has bought a new hat and a new satin gown. She never wants to leave London. She writes that she has been to a reception at the palace and she saw the Prince Regent there, but she wasn't presented to him. She has been to several smart parties, been to tea at the Duchess of Kent's and Grace liked her daughter, Lady Violet, very much. Grace hopes we are well.'

Sarah sighed a little.

'I wish she'd write more about London. Perhaps she will next time.'

It was a month before the next letter came. Again it was Julia who read it aloud.

'Lady Violet is like a sister to me. Lady Violet and I went riding in the park, and we're to be reading Lord Byron's new works from the beginning to end. Lady Violet and I went to Lord Palmer's ball in matching gowns and everyone thought we were sisters. Lady Violet is going to take me to the best dressmaker in town, and I am to stay with Lady Violet while Aunt Octavia is away. I hope you are both well.'

The two sisters were quiet for a while, considering the letter. Then Julia frowned. 'It's odd that Aunt Octavia should go away without Grace.'

'Surely she meant an overnight visit, perhaps while Aunt Octavia visited a sick friend. Aunt cannot leave Grace alone for long.'

'I expect you are right,' Julia agreed and her tone brightened. 'Now, let's have a look at that tulip bulb catalogue from Holland.'

The very next morning, Sarah was to discover how wrong she had been. It was a fine day, and Julia was in the walled garden showing Grimshaw, the gardener, the best way to prune peaches. Sarah was out on the lawn, supervising the housemaids while the feather beds were changed into new ticking covers. She wasn't best pleased when the butler paced his stately way across the feather-covered lawn to say a visitor was at the door.

'Please say I'm not at home, James. You can see how dishevelled I am.'

'I'm afraid that won't be possible, Miss Sarah. The person in question appears to have come from the stage post in Sam Shuttleworth's cart, Miss

Sarah. The quantity of luggage would suggest that she is an invited guest.'

'I'll come at once. Rose, Emily, will you carry on with the last feather bed while I'm away?'

The maids nodded willingly and Sarah hastened indoors to brush goosedown out of her hair! She scampered down the wooden staircase and into the stone-flagged hall. Tewit Manor was looking particularly nice today. The polished flags gleamed like the surface of a moorland stream, reflecting the oak panelling in watery ripples. The battered suit of armour that guarded the hall had been burnished up in a spring clean. Blue and white jugs full of daffodils stood on the oak settles that lined the arched entrance. Sarah's good mood lasted until she popped out through the open door and into the middle of a furious row.

Young Sam Shuttleworth, usually so merry and bright, was crimson in the face and shouting. Sarah hadn't dreamed he would dare raise his voice to a member of the Quality, but there he was shaking his fist and using the most dreadful language.

'Ar, ye old besom! You said you'd gimme a shillen if I got thee here quick. Old Bessie trotted whole way here, and now you offer me a penny!'

A large dark lady wearing an incredibly smart black pelisse with bright scarlet trimmings spoke in a clear, ringing voice.

'I've been here before, my good man, and the fare is one penny.'

She turned away as if the matter was over and advanced upon Sarah like a galleon in full sail.

'And you must be Julia, my dear. How nice to meet you.'

Aunt Octavia! What was she doing here at Tewit Manor?

'Sarah, I'm Sarah,' Sarah muttered, as she was enveloped in a cold and scented handshake.

A copper penny went winging past their heads and pinged on the wall of Tewit Manor as Sam rejected his fare.

Aunt Octavia's thick black eyebrows slanted down in a nasty frown.

'If he can get there quickly for a shilling, he can get here quickly for a penny, and a penny is the correct fare. I absolutely refuse to pay more.'

Sarah looked at Sam's wrathful face and at his poor, exhausted horse. A shilling was a great deal of money and Sam had driven poor Bessie unmercifully.

'Take Bessie to the yard, Sam. Rub her down and get her a drink. I'll be there presently.'

Sam's eyes met hers. He was still flushed with his fury, but Sarah saw in his honest gaze an absolute trust that Miss Sarah would see justice was done, and he turned away, murmuring quietly to his poor horse.

Aunt Octavia behaved as if nothing had happened. She took hold of Sarah's arm in a grip that pinched. Her lips smiled.

'Now, Julia, let's have some tea and get acquainted.'

'Sarah. I'm Sarah, Aunt Octavia,' Sarah repeated.

'So you're little Sarah! I'm sure we are going to be the most marvellous friends.'

Sarah found herself being towed into her own hall, caught fast in a smother of black fabric and red trim. Aunt Octavia stood for a moment sizing up the room and the furniture.

'Sadly old-fashioned,' she proclaimed.

It was James who took Aunt Octavia's outer garments, ordered the boot boy round to the yard to collect the luggage, and ushered both women into the library for tea.

'Thank you, James,' Sarah said. 'And could you send someone to find Miss Julia and warn, that is, inform her that Aunt Octavia is here?'

There was perfect understanding in James's hazel eyes.

'Certainly, Miss Sarah.'

Martha then brought the tea tray.

'Oh, do you still drink Indian tea?' Aunt Octavia enquired. 'It's hardly ever served these days. Could I have a little Madeira?'

'Mother made us all promise never to have alcohol at Tewit Manor.'

Aunt Octavia's tone was scornful.

'How ridiculous! Anyway, she's dead now.'

'Her memory is sacred to us all!' Sarah flared, then she felt hot and uncomfortable — she'd never been rude to a guest before!

Aunt Octavia's muddy brown eyes registered no offence.

'I've brought some very nice sherry for your father. Kindly send a servant to bring in the bottles.'

'I'm sorry, Aunt Octavia, we never allow alcohol into the house.'

'I am in need of refreshment after that journey in that frightful rustic cart.'

'I will have a tisane made for you. Ginger is most effective in cases of travel upset.'

Sarah pulled the bell to summon Martha back to the library, but Aunt Octavia refused to let the subject of alcohol drop.

'But why? Why do you have this ridiculous rule?'

'Because Mother wished it,' Sarah said shortly, but the question made her think.

She'd known since she was little that alcohol was not allowed, but she'd never wondered why. They drank water or lemonade at mealtimes and always had, and Sarah needed no other reason than her promise to her mother. It gave her courage.

'Aunt Octavia, you cannot have your sherry here. So, perhaps you'd rather not stay.'

Sarah's heart thumped in her ears. She could hardly believe her own words. Surely Aunt Octavia would take offence now.

But her aunt simply said, 'How quaint!' and smiled as if nothing had happened.

The latch clicked as Martha entered the library and before Sarah could open her mouth, Aunt Octavia turned to the housekeeper and spoke rudely.

'Fetch me a ginger drink!'

'Yes, ma'am,' the housekeeper replied correctly, but her back spoke volumes as she whisked around the door and settled the latch.

Aunt Octavia leaned forward in her chair as if she and Sarah were the best of friends.

'Now, Sarah, do tell me all about yourself!'

It was a command guaranteed to reduce one to idiocy, Sarah reflected, but luckily Aunt Octavia's next words made it clear that she would much rather talk about herself. Sarah sat back in her chair, nodded her head at intervals and reviewed the situation rapidly. Had she really told a guest to leave? Aunt Octavia didn't look like a woman who'd been rudely asked to leave. She looked perfectly happy as she told Sarah how the Earl of Harbourne had found her yellow muff perfectly charming, like a piece of that yellow thistledown that grows in the south of France.

'Mimosa,' a voice said above their heads. 'It gets very yellow if the weather is dry.'

Sarah looked up gratefully to see Julia smiling at them. She'd taken the time to change and looked perfectly charming. Sarah performed the introductions, but the arrival of another person didn't change Aunt Octavia's conversation. She continued to speak in a loud voice, riding roughshod over Julia's attempts to join in. The two sisters pulled faces at one another until Sarah was threatened with an attack of the giggles and had to excuse herself until dinnertime.

Later that night, as Julia sat brushing her hair by the light of a candle, she reviewed the evening. She spoke aloud to her reflection in the mirror.

'If I'd known what a monster the woman was, I do believe I'd have given Sam Shuttleworth another shilling to cart her away again!'

Dinner had been a nightmare. Their papa was away, and normally the girls would have had a light meal, then sprawled comfortably in the library after dinner. Instead, they had sat in mute and appalled silence, dumb under the flow of Aunt Octavia's monologue.

Julia looked up with a smile as the latch on the bedroom door opened with a click,

'Oh, Sarah, you don't know how much I wanted to see you.'

Sarah came into the room and jumped up on the four-poster.

'I've been here all evening.'

'You might as well not have been. I couldn't say a word to you!'

Sarah nodded. Julia thought how pretty she was. Sarah was not striking in any way, unlike Grace, with her ebony locks and her milk white skin, but she always looked neat and wholesome. Her eyes were a really clear amber, like a moorland stream in the sunlight. Sarah's eyes were luminous with her every thought, and right now they were troubled.

'Whatever could have brought Aunt

Octavia here? And why has she left Grace alone in London?'

'There's no mystery about Grace. Do you really think she'd prefer to come home rather than stay with her fascinating new friend, Lady Violet?'

Sarah looked at her sister with pained eyes.

'I can't think now,' she said sadly, as she stood up to go to her own room. 'My head's thumping worse than it did when I had the measles. Papa is due home in the morning. He'll know what to do. Shall we get up early and ride to meet him?'

Julia felt better as she bade her sister goodnight.

I'm not sure what Papa can do, she told herself, but undoubtedly things will look better in the morning.

2

It seemed strange to have to sneak out of one's own house, but Julia and Sarah moved softly as they donned their riding habits and tiptoed down the creaking wooden stairs to the stables. The old groom, Appleby, was always up early, and he was happy to saddle their ponies in no time.

The two girls clattered under the stone stable arch and turned into the lane that ran past the front of the house. Julia stared at the garden.

'Did it snow last night?'

Sarah was chuckling.

'You know what it is, you wretch. Tell me!' Julia said with a smile.

'I was turning the feather ticks when Aunt Octavia came. I left Rose and Emily to finish the last one, but I'm afraid something went wrong with the process. There are feathers all over the garden.'

Julia snorted with laughter.

It was so good to be out in the open air, laughing, joking, free as two birds. By mutual consent, they didn't mention Aunt Octavia, although once the first freshness was out of the horses, the sisters settled down to a steadier pace and rode side by side so that they could talk.

'What was it you wanted to talk to me about last night, Julia?'

'It's Grimshaw, as usual. How I wish I could sack him!'

'He never seems to learn what you want him to do.'

'It's worse than that,' Julia said. 'He's deliberately obstructive.'

Sarah turned horrified eyes to her sister.

'That can't be right.'

'I've tried telling myself that he's misunderstanding, or that he's naturally slow, but I spent an hour with him yesterday, showing him how to train the peach trees along the south-facing wall of the garden, and when I went to check them, he'd chopped them all down to stumps, ruined them! The more time I spend with him, the more damage he does.'

'He wants to be left alone to smoke his pipe and bully the garden boys,' Sarah said. 'I took some soup down to the cottage and Mrs Grimshaw had walked into a door, again.'

'He hits her!' Julia said. 'What are we to do?'

'We can't sack him,' Sarah declared firmly. 'It would be too cruel to turn his poor wife and children out of the cottage.'

'Oh, Sarah, we won't tell them to leave! You know that, but I do wish I could think of a way of dealing with the man.'

'Don't speak to him.'

'And let him have free run in the garden?'

The sisters fell silent as they considered the problem, but as no solution presented itself, it was a relief to see their father coming into view. When he saw them, he snatched off his hat and waved it vigorously and greeted them with smiling eyes.

'Now this makes a fine morning perfect, so it does! My own lovely daughters come out to meet me. Did you miss your old papa, then?'

'We did, Papa, we did,' the girls assured him.

Julia tried to tell him about Aunt Octavia, but he was bursting with news of his own.

'I called in on Mrs Gregory on the way, and you'll never guess!'

'What, Papa?' Julia asked.

'Toby is home!'

'No!' both of the sisters cried.

This was exciting. Julia tried to remember when they'd last seen him.

'He must have been in India for nearly ten years now.'

'Eleven,' her papa corrected. 'And if Mrs Gregory hadn't assured me herself that it was her own boy returned to him I'd have thought the boy a leprechaun, so changed he is. 'Tis skin and bone, the lad is now. He caught a fever out there. India's no place for an Englishman, by what he was saying. But the lad's done well, if I'm to go by the loot he's brought back with him. You never saw such treasure!'

Descriptions of silk and sandalwood boxes, necklaces, peacock feathers and fans with ivory sticks, along with speculation about Toby's activities in India and his future course of action occupied them delightfully, and it wasn't until they were within sight of Tewit Manor that Julia remembered their visitor. With a nasty lurch in her stomach, she reined in her horse and laid a hand on her papa's arm.

'Just a minute, Papa. We must talk about Aunt Octavia.'

'As soon as he recovers, the lad will be off to London, he tells me. His company has a head office there and they are keeping a place for him. It will seem a mite tame after the excitement of India, I'm thinking.'

'Hush, Papa!' Julia shouted, feeling

really desperate. 'I'm sorry, Papa, but this is so important. It's about Aunt Octavia's visit.'

Her father looked alarmed.

'Oh, that won't be the thing at all!'

Then he looked apologetic.

'It's very strange indeed to be shutting my door to any poor soul, let alone a relative who's a widow, but your Aunt Octavia is no ordinary kind of woman. No, if she's after sending our Gracie back, we'll send the governess down to fetch her. I'll let them have James as well, but Octavia mustn't come here.'

'I'm sorry, Papa, but she's already here.'

'There's nothing to be done then. In the name of glory! Can you be telling me why it should snow on our front lawn and nowhere else in the night?'

Laughing together, they turned towards the house.

Aunt Octavia came swishing over the stone flags to meet them the very second they entered the cool-smelling hall of Tewit Manor. She looked magnificent in a bright blue outfit. She certainly was a good-looking woman.

'My dear Patrick, there's a funny old woman in the best bedroom. I'd be obliged if you'd move her. The room I've been given is rather small.'

Aunt Octavia slipped an arm through Patrick's and looked at him under her lashes with a smile that was clearly meant to be charming, but Patrick shook off her arm and positively roared.

'Old Granny Norah looked after me when I was a baby. Do you think I'd be moving her? I'd sooner send you away, and I think I will. You don't like your room and there isn't another. Be off with you! Get back to London.'

Incredibly, Aunt Octavia was smiling that white toothy smile of hers.

'Oh, Patrick, I had forgotten your quaint Irish manner. No wonder poor Elanora found you so irresistible. There's nobody like you.'

She turned and swept into the morning-room for breakfast. Julia could smell bacon and knew she was hungry, but she stayed put.

'Do you see what she drove me to?' her father was demanding. 'Did you hear what I said to her, girls? Would you believe a man of my age could be so rude? And would you believe that a woman alive could ignore it?'

He tilted his head and listened to the sound of silver clinking on china as Aunt Octavia tucked into kippers and scrambled eggs.

'I'm going to Harrogate on Friday,' he announced.

Julia was about to protest, then she remembered that the trip had indeed been planned some time ago. Sarah took a deep breath. Her flushed cheeks betrayed her agitation, but she spoke calmly.

'Shall we go in to breakfast?'

Now that Mother was dead, it was Sarah who ran Tewit Manor and they all took their orders from her, Julia reflected, as she followed her sister into the breakfast room. It was like Papa to forget himself and storm at Aunt Octavia. It was like Sarah to call them back to order. She was more her mother's daughter than any of them, and Elanora had been from an exquisitely correct English family.

Then Julia remembered that her mother had also been capable of flouting convention. When she'd fallen in love with Patrick Gannon, she'd defied her family in order to marry him, although, of course, there was no question of being outcast from Society, for the Gannons were perfectly respectable landowners with a fine castle near Dublin, accepted wherever they went, Julia had never understood why Elanora's family had been so against them.

From time to time, a Gannon cousin would call by Tewit Manor, as like as not with a pack of mixed hounds and at least ten horses, and she always enjoyed the company of her merry Irish cousins. They were a lot easier to deal with than Aunt Octavia, who had finished eating and was now sipping coffee with relish.

'My dear Patrick, I see you have an invitation to a ball at the Duke of Whitewell's for tomorrow. I look forward to it immensely.'

'The duke always remembers us, but it's out of politeness. He knows I don't care for dancing. Sport, now that's a different matter.'

'But, Patrick, you're surely taking the girls! To do otherwise would be sadly neglectful!'

'I don't think that one of the duke's parties would be at all suitable.'

Julia smothered a smile. The duke's parties, or rather his younger son's parties, were a byword in the district — dancing girls and card games, jugglers and clowns, gipsy fortune tellers and all manner of scandalous goings on. Aunt Octavia was obviously unfamiliar with this particular aristocrat and his reputation!

'Good heavens, Sarah must be nineteen by now. It's almost too late to find a husband for her.'

Patrick's large hand slammed on to

34

the polished table.

'Will you be done with telling me my business, Octavia! Twenty-one is time enough to be putting up their hair and setting down to find husbands!'

'Very well, Patrick, but I'd count it as a very great favour if you would escort me. I'd love to see the castle.'

'I'm not going,' he retorted. 'No amount of coaxing will get me there.'

This time, Julia did see expression in her aunt's eyes. Vicious spite and fury flared for an instant. Later, as the girls were working, or to tell the truth, rather hiding out of the way, in the still-room, she told Sarah her theory.

'That's all she came here for, to go to the duke's. Papa won't go. Perhaps she wants to look for a husband.'

'I can't think that! It's no more than three years since Mr Hamilton died.'

'And it was less than a year after John Wood died that she married Mr Hamilton. I remember that Mother's relatives were shocked. I don't think Mother liked it, to be honest. She loved her brother so much.'

'It must be hard, being a widow,' Sarah said gently.

Julia dropped a kiss on her little sister's cheek.

'To change the subject, dear sister, I want to see Clare Gregory and bring her up to date. Do you want to come with me? Don't forget that Toby's home from India! It will be so exciting to see him.'

'I'll go tomorrow. We'd better take it in turns to be away from home. Goodness knows what might happen at the moment!'

3

In fact, that evening, and the whole of the next day, was quiet and they saw little of Aunt Octavia. Sarah made time to ride over to the Gregorys and was privately much shocked at the thin, sallow young man who sat swathed in cashmere shawls in a big chair by the window.

'I do not think he'll be well enough to take up a post in London any time soon,' she commented to Julia later as the two girls sat embroidering new bed hangings in the big salon with Rose and Emily seated nearby, mending.

'Don't be ridiculous!' Julia snapped. 'He'll be fine in no time at all.'

Sarah gazed at her sister in surprise. There was a flush on her sister's cheeks and her blue eyes were looking anywhere but at her sister's face. A cold sensation crept around Sarah's heart.

Surely not . . . oh, dear Julia. But maybe she was imagining it. Sarah looked at her suspiciously, but what could she say? The click-clack of heels on the floor outside made both girls turn to the door. Aunt Octavia's head popped through the opening.

'All busy with your needles? What a charming sight?' she commented, with no visible signs of being charmed on her face. 'I just wanted to tell you that I'm in charge of dinner tonight. Pheasant and a trifle of my own secret recipe. I so appreciate you having me here and I do think a guest should make a contribution. Dinner tonight shall be mine.'

Aunt Octavia went away briskly, her heels clicking.

'I'd better go and see Cook,' Julia said. 'Life won't be worth living if that woman's upset her.'

But she was back in a very few minutes. She leaned very close so that the two maids couldn't overhear.

'Sarah, whatever do you think? She's

given Cook a whole five shillings! I can't understand it at all.'

Sarah shook out the curtain she was working on and folded it up. Embroidery demanded a tranquil mind and she was feeling too stirred up to concentrate. As she went upstairs to change for dinner she was still puzzling over Aunt Octavia's extraordinary behaviour. She had a foreboding that lay heavy on her and refused to be shaken, although dinner was in fact the most pleasant meal they'd had since Aunt Octavia arrived to disturb the peace at Tewit Manor.

Patrick had regarded his dinner table with bemusement when he walked into the room. It was dressed with trailing leaves of ivy, gold candles and bows of red ribbon.

'What kind of trumpery and frippery is this?' he yelled.

But as course succeeded delicious course, he mellowed considerably. Aunt Octavia, too, was behaving differently. She hung on Patrick's every utterance and encouraged him to talk about himself. Papa was enjoying himself hugely. He was in full spate now with one of his hunting stories.

Julia leaned over and whispered in Sarah's ear, 'Papa's very red.'

Sarah looked at her sister and saw that the blue eyes were worried. Her cheeks were as pink as her father's. The room must be warmer than usual. Sarah touched her own warm face and realised that she was feeling quite light headed. She suddenly felt happy as Aunt Octavia called to James to bring the coffee pot to the table.

'My own special recipe,' she said, pouring Papa a cup. 'We ladies will retire now, and leave Mr Gannon to drink his in peace.'

Aunt Octavia swept them out and into the library. The fire flickered in the draught as they opened the door. Sarah found herself giggling as she walked in and threw herself on to the leather sofa. Julia threw herself down next to her sister, bouncing a little. Sarah found this exquisitely funny, and she had a laughing fit that ended in an attack of hiccups.

She picked up her book from the polished wood table. She'd been looking forward to a chapter all day, but she couldn't concentrate and she threw it down again. Julia wasn't faring much better with her seed catalogue.

'The print is so terrible small,' she complained. 'Shall we play cards instead? Do you like whist, Aunt Octavia?'

Their aunt stood up and her brown eyes were unreadable.

'I left my vinaigrette on the table.'

Julia stared owlishly as the door closed behind Aunt Octavia.

'She's usually quick enough to call a servant to fetch for her.'

Sarah was still struggling with hiccups.

'Oh, I do feel peculiar.'

'I feel quite jolly.' Julia laughed. 'Come here and let me pat your back, you baby, you.'

Having her back patted was soothing

and Sarah smiled dreamily.

'Aunt Octavia's food was very rich. I'm feeling quite sleepy.'

Julia yawned and snuggled into the tapestry cushions of the sofa.

'Shall we play cards?'

'I'll fetch them in just a minute,' Sarah said, but the fire crackled and she could feel herself sinking into the comfort of the tapestry cushions.

Sarah's heavy lids fluttered over her eyes and she slipped into a happy golden daydream. She wasn't asleep, really, aware of the fire and her sister beside her, but she thought only a few minutes had passed, yet here was James, arranging the tea tray with a meaningful clatter.

Sarah sat up and clutched her aching head. She'd had more headaches this week than she normally did in a year. Her sister groaned beside her.

'It's so bright in here! It's hurting my eyes.'

The little gold clock chimed ten. Sarah felt startled.

'Where is Papa? He never came into the library.'

Julia said, 'Perhaps he went to smoke a pipe with Appleby.'

James made no reply, but he put down the tea things and glided smoothly from the room.

'James will find him,' Julia said, yawning hugely. 'I do feel peculiar.'

'I think Aunt Octavia's dinner was too rich,' Sarah said, touching her own throbbing head.

She looked at her sister. Julia's cheeks were as white now as they had been pink at dinner.

'Do you want a herbal tisane?'

'I'd be sick,' Julia said, clutching her stomach. 'Let's just go to bed.'

Despite her doze on the sofa, and the unpleasant feeling in her stomach, Sarah went to sleep directly. It was a strange, heavy sleep, shot through with bad dreams. When she heard a tapping at the wood of her bedroom door, it was hard to wake up.

It wasn't unusual for Sarah to be

woken in the night. If a maid was to have toothache, it would always be at three in the morning. She opened the door, to see James.

'What time is it?' she asked.

'Around five, Miss Sarah.'

Sarah shivered in the cold air from the passage.

'Is somebody ill?'

Now she could see that James was still in his day clothes, and his dark frockcoat was somewhat dishevelled. A nasty shock zinged over her as she saw that James had a bruise on his cheek.

'Is it Papa?'

James gestured for her to follow him.

'In the library, Miss Sarah.'

Sarah could feel her heart pounding as she followed James's broad back down the draughty passage that led to the stairs. A hundred questions boiled up inside her, but not one of them passed her lips, and she knew she was afraid of the answers.

The fire was out, and the room was cold and dishevelled. By the light of the candles that she and James were carrying, she could see that her papa was sitting on one of the leather sofas, leaning forward with his head in his hands. His clothes were awry and his shock of white hair was disordered.

'Papa?' she questioned.

Her only answer was a deep and heartfelt groan. Sarah turned to James.

'James, call one of the maids. No, better wake Martha. Ask her to get the fire made up and to bring us some fresh candles. We shall want a hot drink. Tea would be best, I think. Also, bring Papa's dressing-gown and a cloth and some hot water. Fetch me the small bottle of arnica from the kitchen.'

The bustle that resulted was soothing. Sarah was able to ward off the sense of foreboding that threatened to make her hands shake and her heart shrivel while she was busy, but not for long. As she bent over her papa to wash his face and tend the nasty graze on his forehead, she couldn't help noticing the mixture of fumes that hung about him, also his queer, shamefaced expression.

'Papa, how did you hurt your face?'

Her papa gave a faint smile.

'James hit me.'

Her brain absolutely refused to believe her ears.

'Papa, what happened?'

'It happened as I said, child, and don't look so shocked. I hit him first. Got him a good one, too.'

In all her years, Papa and James had been more like friends than man and master. Sarah knew that they'd been through some kind of adventure together.

'You have to tell me what happened, Papa!'

His eyes refused to meet hers.

'There's no easy way to tell you this. I went to the duke's last night.'

'You were drinking?' she guessed.

Her papa nodded his head miserably and Sarah tried to process the knowledge. Lots of fine gentlemen drank all the time and it did them no harm, she knew that. Their own family was unusual in its temperance. Yet she knew in her bones that it went deeper than that with her father — hints, half-heard words that had made no sense at the time, secrets that she'd known all along, really, but never needed to face before now.

'You promised mother never to drink,' she said slowly.

'I've a weakness with the drink, it's true. Your mother wouldn't marry me unless I swore to her by all I held holy that I'd never touch a drop again, and she had the right of it! For look what's happened the very first time I broke my vow.'

Sarah wanted to smooth away the misery that smothered him.

'But you'll never do it again, Papa. We'll forget it ever happened.'

'It won't be as easy as that, child. When an Irishman drinks, he gambles, and when I take a wager there's nothing will hold me back. They were playing at the castle last night. I gambled with all that I had, and I lost it.'

'Lost it?' Sarah echoed. 'Lost all your money?'

'Money? I wish that were all. Everything, I said, and everything I meant. We'll have to go back to Ireland, and think how that makes me feel! A man of my age crawling back to his family. Go on! Go on with you. You'd better wake up your sister and tell her to pack. As from today, this is our home no longer. I've lost Tewit Manor as well.'

4

Sarah would never forget the walk up the stairs to her sister's room. She felt as if she were perched over an abyss, the solid ground beneath her feet quicksand.

Julia didn't wake as Sarah entered the room. Sarah kneeled at the fireplace and lit a quick fire on top of the ashes of the old one. Then she drew the curtains. The sky was just a little lighter. Dawn on a wet March day didn't offer much in the way of light.

Julia stirred in the bed.

'Sarah? Am I late? I don't feel myself this morning, and there's a terrible taste in my mouth.'

'Just lie still a minute. I can hear Martha bringing you some tea.'

As the gloomy old housekeeper entered the room, Sarah studied her face. The servants would know everything by now.

'Weary load, Miss Sarah. Weary load,' she said, plonking down the tray, but her eyes seemed no more depressed than usual.

Julia's eyes were puzzled and she rubbed them hard as she took in the fire and the tea and the unusual fact that her sister was in her room at all.

'Am I ill? What a fool question! I feel strange, that's for sure. But, Sarah, something is up? What is it?'

Sarah took a cup of tea for herself and the heat and the freshness of it was like medicine. The feeling of physical relief was temporary, however, for not only would the situation not go away, but the news had to be broken to her sister. Julia seemed principally concerned with their papa on hearing.

'To break his vow to Mother! But whatever made him do it? There's no drink in the house even if he did suddenly want to get drunk, and I can't see him getting out the horses and setting off to the duke's unless he was drunk already. Sarah!'

She looked at her sister with eyes that were blazing.

'Aunt Octavia! She brought some bottles of sherry with her, remember? Only you wouldn't let her bring them in to the house. Now I know why she prepared a special meal last night! Remember how red Papa's face was? And how we felt so queer and then fell asleep? Aunt Octavia must have laced all the food with alcohol. She started Papa drinking and then talked him into going to the duke's, because for some reason of her own, she was determined to go to the castle.'

'It's not possible!' Sarah cried, knowing in her heart that her sister had the right of it. 'She couldn't have been so wicked!'

'Oh, couldn't she?' Julia demanded grimly. 'I'm going to see her. Now!'

'But the house . . . ' Sarah cried, pattering after her sister towards the guest room. 'We have to decide where we are going to live. We need to think what's to be done.'

Julia waved aside domestic matters. 'Aunt Octavia first.'

She knocked on the wooden panelling of the door but she didn't wait for an answer. She lifted the latch and marched in, Sarah just behind her. One pace into the room, they both stopped, astonished. A large fire blazed in the hearth. Candles burned in every sconce, and in two candelabra that had been brought up from the hall. In the midst of all this light and glitter, Aunt Octavia was pacing the room in a cherry-red dressing-gown. Heaps of clothes in strong bright colours lay about the room. Two large trunks gaped open on the bed. Then Sarah saw Emily and Rose, both busy packing.

'Leaving, Aunt Octavia?' Julia asked.

The face Aunt Octavia turned towards them was as bright as the room with all its candles. For once her expression was clear in her eyes. Happiness and a blazing triumph were writ there.

'I must get to London at once. The dear, dear Marquis of Blackburn has asked me to dine at his house. Such an honour, such an event. I'll need a new gown. I must leave at once. The maids tell me the carter is on his way.'

Sarah caught a sight of Julia's face and knew that her sister's temper was rising. Sarah spoke to the maids hastily.

'Run downstairs and see if Sam's coming. Quickly now, both of you.'

Julia didn't notice the maids leave. She was looking at Aunt Octavia as if the woman was a new kind of vermin that she was just about to exterminate from her garden, and a spot of colour burned red in each cheek.

'So that's what you came here for,' she said slowly. 'And when Papa wouldn't take you to the duke's so you could scrape an acquaintance with his fine friends, you got Papa drunk. You sneaked alcohol into his food to start him drinking, and do you know, Aunt Octavia, I believe that you know why Papa shouldn't drink. You were there when he married my mother. You must have known that he had a weakness.'

The joy on Aunt Octavia's face was hard to witness when Sarah felt so shattered. The woman was unmoved by Julia's scorn and her accusations.

'It's not my fault if Patrick lost his head. I didn't get him drunk. He was shouting for more quickly enough. I can't be blamed if he won't stop drinking once he's got the taste. Your mother was a fool to marry him. A gentleman should be able to hold his drink and keep his gambling in check as well. Have you never wondered why you came to live in this benighted part of Yorkshire. Your mother knew she wouldn't be able to control him, promise or not, if she took him back to Ireland with that pack of drinking, card-playing brothers of his. She made him swear not to drink or gamble and then she carried him off to the most remote part of the country she could think of. She should have chosen her husband more carefully. He disgraced her in the end, just as I prophesied.'

'Only because you tricked him into

starting to drink!' Julia cried in a shaking voice. 'I want you out of here, you deceitful woman. And I want you to send Grace back. You're not fit to associate with a pure young girl.'

Incredibly, the light in Aunt Octavia's face didn't dim. She was still blazingly happy and Julia's condemnation was nothing to her, yet perhaps at some level she was hurt, because she hit back as hard as she could.

'You can see that I'm packing, and I'm not likely to come back. As for Grace, she'll come back when she's ready. She's to come to the marquis's dinner with me, and I doubt if she'd chose to miss that. And there's another thing, Miss High and Mighty, that you don't seem to have thought of. Where shall I send her? You two are homeless vagabonds now!'

'Homeless maybe, but honourable!' Julia replied shortly, but Sarah could see from the agony in her eyes that the shot had gone home.

The anger in her eyes leaked away to

be replaced by misery, and there was nothing that Sarah could do to make her feel better. Losing everything didn't just mean houses and money and horses. It meant losing peace, security, the power to make people happy. All these had been ripped away by a woman who had already turned away from them.

'Where have those maids got to?'

Rose opened the door as Aunt Octavia was speaking.

'If you please, ma'am, Sam's sent word that he's busy. There's only the pig cart if you want to catch today's stagecoach.'

Aunt Octavia hesitated.

'That won't do at all. Very well. Go back and book Sam for tomorrow and change my ticket as well. I'll send a note down to London. My maid should be better by now and Celine's very clever. She knows the type of gown that suits me. She can begin work on the shell and trim it when I arrive. Fetch me some writing paper at once.'

'Wait, Rose!' Julia thundered. 'Order the pig cart! She is leaving today.'

She swung round on Aunt Octavia with contempt blazing in her eyes.

'If you need to stay in Yorkshire, you can stay with your fine friends. After what you did to Papa, I won't have you in our house a second longer.'

Aunt Octavia was starting to look ruffled.

'I've decided to go back anyway, and I shouldn't be so rude about my friends. Who do you think owns this house now?'

Sarah was dumbfounded. She hadn't got past the thought that the house was lost to them. It had never occurred to her to visualise a new owner! Aunt Octavia seemed satisfied by the effect her words had produced. Her eyes were so full of spite and a vicious kind of triumph that Sarah recoiled before them. And her next words were even worse.

'My friend, the Marquis of Blackburn, that's who. Your precious papa lost everything to the marquis, my special friend, the marquis, and if he were to marry, then his wife would share in all his property, including any little hovel that he might have picked up in a card game.'

Julia was trembling all over.

'You disgust me!' she cried in a low, shaking voice. 'I'll speak to you no longer. Rose, Emily, get this woman packed as soon as you can and I'll send James to make sure she gets to the stagecoach.'

Sarah could see the shadowy forms of the household servants at every window as she stood on the gravel sweep in front of the house. The garden staff were busy in the rose beds and the stable boys were peeping through the arch of the yard as the pig cart rumbled over the gravel and stopped at the front door. Aunt Octavia, looking magnificent in emerald silk, swept out and turned to face the sisters, but before she could open her mouth, Julia was on her.

'Leave!' she said shortly.

Flushing slightly, Aunt Octavia climbed up into the cart. There was a push and a bustle as those servants who'd managed to find a legitimate reason for being on the scene scrambled to throw up her boxes and cases, and then Appleby, who had obliged for the occasion but didn't look very happy about it, clicked his tongue at his bay cob, and the pig cart jolted and swayed through the gates.

'Good riddance!' Julia said clearly, oblivious to her audience. 'We'll sell that cart tomorrow, now that the last pig's left the premises.'

Sarah had never felt so wretched. She took her sister's arm and led her into the house, speaking softly into her ear.

'We'll have to sell everything,' she said. 'Sell or pack. But I don't know where we are going. So I don't know what to take.'

'Are you sure Papa said we must leave today?' Julia asked. 'The thing's impossible! Surely they'll give us time to find another house.'

'I'll find Papa,' Sarah replied. 'It was hard enough accepting that he'd gambled the house away. I was in no state to start making plans.'

She felt sick every time the bitter impact of leaving Tewit Manor came to mind, but still, the servants must be organised. No matter whose house it was, it must be cleaned and the people in it fed.

Julia fled, to her garden, she said, but Sarah saw her heading off on her horse in the direction of the Gregory house. Her heart ached for her sister. If her suspicions were true and Julia was forming an attachment with Toby, how would this move affect her sister? It was another problem to think about as Sarah chivvied the staff back to their daily routine. They asked her no direct questions, for which she was truly grateful. They were entitled to know what was happening as soon as possible, but first she had to find out what that was.

As soon as she felt she could leave

them, Sarah went to find her papa. James, who had changed into fresh livery and was looking so tidy you'd never have known anything had happened, until you saw the bruises on his face, was just coming out of her father's room, closing the door softly behind him, holding the latch so it didn't click.

'James,' Sarah began, and then she halted, feeling helpless.

She'd known James all her life, but she'd never really known him, she realised now. She looked up at his calm face and steady hazel eyes and felt better. She had the comforting feeling that whatever was to happen, James could be relied upon.

'Your father's asleep now. We'll talk in the library,' he told her.

Once they were settled and private, Sarah turned to him and met his eyes frankly.

'James, I don't know what to do.'

Once again, she found comfort in the steadiness of his expression.

'I believe that your father is planning

to return to his family in Ireland.'

'So he said. But, James, we've never been there!'

Hot tears, the first that Sarah had shed, overwhelmed her, but they didn't make her feel better. The steel knot in her throat only tightened its grip. James let her cry for a few minutes before he spoke, and when he did, there was a lack of sympathy in his tone that was bracing.

'You'll have a good home.'

Sarah struggled to subdue the painful gulping sobs that only tore at her insides. Finally, she managed to speak.

'I believe the Marquis of Blackburn is the new owner of our house, from today, Papa said, but what does that mean to us?'

'The marquis may be the new owner, but I would have thought a period of grace before we vacate would be acceptable. He is leaving for London today, at first light he said, so you could send a letter to ask him. Have Mr Mellor draft a legal letter, suggesting a date to be agreed mutually.'

Sarah felt some of her panic and shakiness retreat.

'James, you are a marvel! Of course we can't leave today, and I never thought of asking Mellor's advice at all. I'll send Rose for Mr Mellor at once, and he shall write a letter. And then . . . '

She trailed off and looked at James hopefully. The oddness of looking to the butler for help touched the back of her mind and was gone. These were desperate times, and James was unexpectedly resourceful.

'Wait until your papa wakes up for the next step,' he suggested now. 'I expect he'll have some plan in mind. Most likely you'll stay with your relatives for a while, and then arrange to rent a house nearby.'

Rent a house! The concept sprang fully-formed into Sarah's mind, blazing. Rent a house, of course, that was what people did. Papa had been forever riding off to see people about their rents. Well, Papa was no longer a landlord, but why shouldn't he be a tenant? She couldn't imagine that the Marquis of Blackburn would want to live in Tewit Manor himself, so why shouldn't he let it to them?

She thought over the idea quickly and found it perfect. If only for a year, it would give them time to all become accustomed to the new state of affairs. A passionate determination to make it happen seized her. She didn't want to go to Ireland. She wanted to stay here. She looked at James quickly.

'The marquis is going to London, you say?'

'He was calling for breakfast as I took your papa home.'

Sarah thought of Aunt Octavia and wondered if the pig cart had made it to the inn where the stagecoach stopped. The heavy, ponderous vehicle left at ten and it was several days to London. It was always full.

'But the marquis wouldn't take the stage, would he?'

'No. He has a fine carriage of his own.'

'Then he'll stop at The Swan for lunch. Carriages always do.'

Even now, James was too correct to ask his mistress where she was going, but he looked at her with such intensity that Sarah relented. After all he'd done for them, he deserved her confidence.

'I'm going to see the marquis in person. We can't just turn out of our home, and besides, I don't want to. I want to rent Tewit Manor for a year at least while we decide what's to be done.'

'A good plan, but couldn't Mr Mellor frame the request in his letter?'

It was a sound suggestion, she knew it was, but Sarah was desperate. To sit down with the lawyer and compose a letter was beyond her whirling brain. She realised at once that she wanted to gallop across the fields. The freedom would make her feel better.

'If I cut across the fields, I should be able to catch him. You know the road goes the very long way round. A letter would take such ages. It could be several weeks before we hear. I couldn't stand the waiting.'

James nodded thoughtfully, and again there was respect in his eyes.

'As you wish, Miss Sarah.'

5

It was pure pleasure to be out in the open air and moving, although it was a raw, damp day with a wind that cut like a knife. Sarah gave Dapple her head, and the old grey mare galloped freely for the first few minutes at least, although she soon slowed to a canter.

'You darling!' Sarah told her mare, patting the grey neck.

Then she felt the pit of her stomach tremble again. Whom did Dapple belong to now? For a few seconds Sarah would forget the queerness and uncertainty of her life, then she'd be reminded again. Everything was different now. As she entered a dark green plantation planted with new baby pine trees, her gaze fell on a **Private Wood** sign with a feeling of horror. This wasn't her wood any more. She was trespassing!

Going across the fields to The Swan was at least eight miles shorter than going by road, and the marquis's carriage would not move as quickly over the rutted lane as Dapple over the fields, but she couldn't relax.

If I miss the man, I can have Mellor write to him, she told herself. But she didn't want to wait for a letter to be sent and then wait for a reply. She wanted her life settled now, and she was tense and uncomfortable until she came within sight of the fine old coaching inn and saw a smart carriage outside it. Good, the marquis was still inside.

One problem over, the next reared its head at once. What on earth was she to say to the man? Her knees shook and her resolve faltered, and nothing less than losing her home would have driven her on. Johnson, the owner of the inn, came out to meet her, his eyes curious, and even a little censorious.

'Why, Miss Sarah, what can have brought thee here? And all alone!'

She smiled at the man as casually as she could.

'I have a letter from Papa from the marquis. That is his carriage, isn't it? May I see the marquis, please?'

'I don't know, Miss Sarah, and that's the truth. He's a queer 'un, the marquis, and he don't like disturbing. Well, he pays me extra to see to it.'

Sarah put a hand on the innkeeper's solid arm.

'Can you send someone to ask him if he will see me? Please, Johnson?'

The expression in his eyes softened as he looked down at her.

'Little bit of a thing, aren't thee? Aye, well, I'll send in Ted to ask him.'

He whistled shrilly and a grinning lad popped into being beside them. Johnson explained what was to be done, and the boy went off. She shook and shivered as she waited, but luckily the boy was back in a few seconds.

'He says to go on in, like.'

Johnson showed her to a private parlour at the side of the building.

Sarah was so nervous as she entered the room that her vision went all blurry. It was a relief to find herself sitting on a mahogany chair upholstered in green velvet. Now at least she wouldn't fall over. She'd never been so frightened in all her happy, sheltered life, but if she were to buy them a breathing space, her request must be made.

She was being stared at, she found, by a man who looked so extraordinary that she knew he must be very fashionable. His eyes were slanted, dark and bloodshot. His hair was dark and curled over his shoulders, his clothes were as bright as Aunt Octavia's, and he was looking at her with malicious amusement.

'My dear, I think I can guess what this little visit is about! You are the gambler's beautiful daughter, are you not? How perfectly wonderful. One never expects such sensational events to happen to one in real life.'

Sarah struggled hard to comprehend him.

'Finding it hard?' the marquis suggested sweetly, but she knew there was no sympathy in this man at all. 'My dear, allow me to make it easy for you. I accept your very generous offer.'

He held out a hand. Sarah looked at the soft white skin, the rings on his fingers and the lace that fell all around it and she would sooner have picked up a slug with her bare hands than touch this man.

'I don't know how much I should offer,' she stammered, wishing she knew more about the business of renting property.

Malice glinted in the marquis's eyes.

'Why, your young and lovely person, of course, in exchange for your family home. There's a room upstairs. Come! Why should we wait?'

Sarah stared at the man and hated him. She spoke as formally as she could and prayed that she got the legal terminology correct.

'You are mistaken in your supposition. I have come to request that my family might take a lease upon Tewit Manor, for a year at least. We cannot vacate the property immediately, nor should we be expected to.'

The marquis dropped his hand. His good humour didn't seem to abate, but Sarah had the feeling he was the most dangerous man she'd ever come across. He was like a steel blade, cool and polished on the outside, even elegant, but capable of cutting deep if he touched you the wrong way.

'What a shame! It's been a long while since I bedded such a pure and pretty maid. Come, sleep with me and I'll return your old home to you.'

'I'll only discuss a lease.'

'Now that your father has gambled away all your money, are you sure you are in a position to turn down such an excellent exchange?'

Sarah stood up.

'Sir, I came here to request a year's rental to enable us to put matters in order before we went to my father's family in Ireland. If you are not willing to discuss the lease with me, I shall leave.'

The marquis shrugged as he accepted defeat.

'I no longer have the deeds.'

'But you won Tewit Manor from Papa at cards, did you not?'

'Indeed I did, but I have made them over to Whitewell in order to settle an old debt.'

The old duke now owned Tewit Manor! The ownership of her beloved house was passing around the county as casually as if it were a gold coin, and the marquis was even more corrupt than she'd thought. He was capable of ruining a woman for nothing. She met his sly gaze directly.

'Sir, you are no gentleman.'

He was unmoved.

'And it is a very great shame that you are still a lady. I would have enjoyed it immensely.'

Sarah walked briskly down the smoky, oak-lined corridor of the inn and burst out into the fresh air. The young lad was walking Dapple. He took the mare to the mounting block and Sarah took her seat gladly. Dapple turned her head for home, and every fibre of Sarah's being longed to let her go, but instead, she turned the mare's head towards the village and the twin lodges that guarded the two-mile drive that led to Whitewell Castle.

6

To Sarah's relief, her reception at Whitewell Castle went smoothly. There was no sign of the son or any of his wild guests. She was shown into a formally-furnished room which had the most delightful views over the lawns and parkland of the castle and then the rolling hills that lay beyond. She was hardly kept waiting at all before the elderly butler returned.

'His Grace will see you now.'

The old duke was in a room on the ground floor that was so big that you hardly noticed a four-poster bed with gorgeously embroidered hangings in one corner. He was sitting in an invalid's wicker chair next to a window that overlooked the park. His blue eyes were faded. There was such a sad air about him and he looked so frail and old-fashioned in his wig and starched linen, that Sarah found it easy to approach him. He listened to her tangled story with gentle good manners and at the end he patted her hand kindly.

'My dear, I'm sorry for all you've been through, but I don't think I can help you. I am not aware of being the owner of Tewit Manor, but let me check.'

He made a slight motion with his finger and one of the footmen stationed by the door leaped forward.

'Will you ask Stanton to attend me?'

His eyes were kind as he smiled at Sarah.

'My agent takes care of business for me these days.'

Sarah felt warmly towards this gentle, kindly man. She could see that arthritis had bent his fingers, and the skin was flaking very badly.

'How do you keep?' she asked shyly.

'I do very well,' he assured her, 'so long as I take several hot baths a day. Then I remain pretty comfortable.'

'It must dry your skin. Would you not consider a lotion in the water?'

'And smell like a perfumed powder puff? No thank you.'

'I'll send you a herbal lotion that smells right for a man,' Sarah promised. 'Fresh and a little medicinal. My sister grew the plants herself.'

The sad expression in the duke's eyes lifted slightly.

'That would be most kind, especially if you would consider bringing your potion in person. The days can be a little slow, confined to this chair.'

'Of course, I will,' Sarah said.

The agent, who was very stiff and correct and seemed to have all the grandeur that the duke lacked, arrived, and the duke explained the situation.

'Your Grace is absolutely correct in his supposition. I did indeed acquire the manor and holdings of Tewit Manor on his behalf. The farms are minuscule, but as they border Your Grace's property, I thought they would be a sound investment.'

'How much did we pay for it?'

'Money as such did not enter the equation. If Your Grace would endeavour to cast his mind back to the business of Blackburn and the equine that passed away in suspicious circumstances shortly after purchase, he will remember that Blackburn promised to recompense the loss incurred on that occasion, and that also there were some notes of hand given in respect of a game of chance undertaken between Blackburn and Your Grace's youngest son.'

Sarah saw a glint of anger which was soon replaced by the duke's usual expression of sadness. For all his wealth and grand position, she felt sorry for the man. He suffered such ill health, and the whole county knew what a bad lot his son was.

'I wish you to draw up a lease for Tewit Manor so that Mr Patrick Gannon and his family may rent it for as long as they wish for the sum of, oh, let's say seventy-five pounds per year.'

Stanton looked most unhappy.

'Your Grace should be advised that the property in question would be capable of realising a far great sum if it were to be marketed in a more advantageous fashion.'

The duke had only lifted one eyebrow but Stanton choked to a halt.

'Yes, Your Grace. At once, Your Grace.'

The duke turned to Sarah as the man left the room.

'He's a good agent,' he said, smiling at her.

Sarah could see pain and exhaustion in his eyes. Two menservants with the look of nurses now entered the room, followed by a doctor in a frockcoat. The duke made no attempt to pretend that he wasn't glad to see them, yet he turned to Sarah with real warmth in his eyes, to say goodbye.

'Thank you so much,' she told him. 'You have my family's deepest gratitude, and I promise to return with the moisturising lotion.'

'The thanks are all mine,' he assured her. 'It's not often I spend the afternoon with such a charming companion.'

As Sarah rode home, she didn't know how she felt. She was hungry, shaky, confused. So much had happened in such a short time. She felt a lump in her throat as she rode around the bend in the road where Tewit Manor came into sight. She loved the old grey buildings so much.

Everything was changed, but her family could at least stay put while they decided what to do next. As she turned into the stable yard, she was met by so many dogs and so many horses that for a bewildered minute she thought the local hunt was meeting at her house. Then she saw a young man in a splendid driving coat of many capes.

'Connor?' she called. 'Is that you?'

The young man turned laughing eyes towards her.

'As ever was, me darling cousin. How are you?'

It was difficult to know where to

start, but by the time the animals were settled and they were both in the house taking refreshments, Sarah had choked out most of the story. Connor seemed to take it very lightly.

'Uncle George was just the same. Once he'd had a drink there was no holding him back. Why, he gambled his own wife away once. 'Twas in the old days, of course, when you could buy a woman at market. She was probably better off without him. The drink carried him off soon afterwards. A blessing in disguise, really, for he was in a fair way to ruin the family.'

'How can you laugh about it?'

'Might as well laugh as cry, and it's a fact that every so often a Gannon is born who cannot hold his drink at all. George was one, your papa is another. Don't be worrying yourself about it, cousin. I could never understand why you wanted to live in this county in the first place, when there's rooms going begging at the castle. Don't be shy about it. Pack up and come to us. We'd love to have you.'

His easy hospitality was comforting.

'Thank you, Connor. We may do so in future, but for now the duke has granted a lease so that we can stay at Tewit Manor for a while.'

Her papa entered as she spoke.

'And how are we to be paying for a lease, daughter?'

Sarah felt cold all over as she looked at her father's flushed and angry face. She'd been through so much to secure the lease that it hurt to have her efforts dismissed, and then she saw the shame and the sadness in his blue eyes and realised that he was blustering to cover his uncomfortable feelings.

'You'll think of something, Papa,' she assured him. 'You know you will.'

'Come to Ireland!' Connor urged again.

Sarah heard Julia arriving and realised that it was dinner time. She rushed upstairs to change, leaving her cousin doing his best to persuade Patrick Gannon to return to Ireland. The topic continued over dinner.

Julia wanted to stay put, which strengthened Sarah's suspicions about Toby Gregory, because Julia had more than once expressed a fancy to see Ireland, Connor was mad for them to move to the castle at once, and their papa didn't seem to know what he wanted.

''Tis the rent that's worrying me,' he finally confessed. 'We've nothing at the moment beyond the little bit your mother left you girls.'

'At the moment,' Sarah said thoughtfully. 'Could you make it grow, Papa? Couldn't we find some way to make money?'

'Don't tease me,' he grumbled. 'My head's hurting. Tell me instead, Connor, how's everyone at home now?'

'They are all well, and beg to be remembered to you. I have a long list in my luggage, Miss Sarah, for your herbal concoctions. Seems like everyone in the family has placed an order for something. I'll be carrying the contents of a shop back with me, so I will.'

'A shop . . . ' Sarah mused.

'Aye, they won't be having any of that stuff from Dublin, or even London any more. Sarah's herbs or nothing, that's what they say to me. My mama did see the length of the list, by the way, and there's a little present in my luggage. She also told me that I was to ask you if there was anything she could send you in return.'

'Why, I don't think so,' Sarah murmured, but her thoughts were busy.

Only the last time she'd been shopping, she'd been shocked at the price charged for shampoos and soaps and perfumed lotions.

'Where do shopkeepers get the lotions that they sell?' she enquired.

Julia's eyes met hers. They were wide with shock, as she understood Sarah's meaning.

'From people like us,' she replied slowly, 'who grow the herbs, mix up the potions, and then sell them to the shops.'

Later that night, Julia sat curled up

on Sarah's bed, hugging her knees thoughtfully.

'We have to get money from some-where.'

'I know nothing about money, do you? Papa said we had some money from Mama.'

'I don't know how much it is, or how the capital is invested, but our allowances come from money that Mama left us, in our names.'

Sarah felt wretched.

'It's so hard to think about. Maybe we should just go to Ireland and let the family look after us.'

'No. It would be very bad for Papa to do that. You know why.'

'But our allowances are so small! How can we pay for the rent and the horses and the servants, and food and I don't know what else besides?'

Julia smiled at her sister.

'Don't worry about it now, Sarah. We'll find out all these things and learn about economy as we go along, and maybe about trade, too. I thought your idea was a good one. We could always ask Toby for advice.'

Sarah cast a look at Julia. Her sister's cheeks were pink and blushing.

'Toby knows all about buying and selling. That's what India merchants do. He'll help us.'

'We'd better see what Papa says.'

'Get into bed, Sarah, and we'll worry about it tomorrow. Maybe you could ask the duke for advice on how to make money.'

7

The duke seemed fascinated by Sarah's tale on her next visit. He kept the bottle of bath lotion close at hand as they conversed, inhaling the scent with evident pleasure in between the many questions he asked her.

'It's getting late in the year for planting,' he observed finally. 'You'll have to set seed straight away if you are to produce any amount of herbs.'

Sarah couldn't help laughing.

'How does a grand person like you know anything about seeds?'

The duke smiled at her and his eyes shone with gentle amusement.

'My agent and my farmers report to me, you know. I wouldn't be able to judge how they were running my affairs if I were ignorant.'

'You don't seem at all shocked at the idea of our entering trade. Yet Papa is so much against it.'

The duke inhaled the herbal fragrance of the bath essence once more.

'The smell alone is so refreshing,' he murmured softly. 'If it does half as much good for my skin as it does my spirits, I'll be eternally grateful. Why should you not spread your expertise, my dear? You can make people feel better and support yourself into the bargain. Oh, I know what you are asking, and is it a wise question. Society will indeed ostracise you. You and your sister may never get husbands. Does that trouble you?'

'No. I suspect that my sister, and this is a secret, Your Grace, but I suspect that my sister is in a fair way to falling for a man who is a merchant himself. She says he will help us in our adventure.'

'And yourself?'

Sarah met his laughing blue eyes.

'I do not plan to marry.'

The doctor and the male nurses entered the room at that moment.

'I never knew an afternoon pass so fast. My dear, will you return and keep an old man company?' the duke said wistfully.

'With pleasure,' Sarah assured him.

Her papa did not seem much impressed by the duke's blessing for their idea of selling herbal lotions when she told him on her return to the manor.

'He is so grand that nothing could affect his place in Society. It's a different matter for the penniless Gannon girls.'

As usual, it was Julia who dared to stand up to their father.

'If we went ahead with our business, we wouldn't be penniless!'

Patrick Gannon banged on the table sharply.

'We'll have no such wild talk in my house!' he thundered, and slammed out of the room in a temper.

'Oh, dear,' Sarah murmured.

'He's softening,' Julia prophesied. 'You know, Sarah, your duke was right about seed. I had better send for more and sow what I already have.'

'But Papa forbade us!'

'Don't look so worried, sweetheart. If we don't need the plants then no harm done, and if we do, why, they'll all be ready. Will you come to the Gregorys' tonight? I want you to hear what Toby has to say about packets and bottles. He says we need a name for our company.'

As soon as she saw Toby, the words just burst out of Sarah.

'Toby! You don't look like the same man! How well you seem.'

Toby's smile lit up his face.

'Thanks to Miss Julia's herbs and my mother's home cooking.'

The whole atmosphere of the house was different. Although a couple of fine cashmere shawls still lay at the ready in case Toby relapsed, a table full of papers stood next to him and he was obviously working. It wasn't just that Toby was looking so much better and was now promoted from the invalid chair to the sofa, there was an atmosphere of hustle and bustle about the whole house. Builders hammered and whistled in the kitchen, new rugs gleamed on the floors, and both Mrs Gregory and Clare were sporting new gowns.

Now Sarah could see what Julia saw in Toby. She could see the charm of his expression and the good sense that smiled from his eyes. A little conversation made her realise how clever he was. He seemed to understand every nuance of trade, and tried to talk her through each one.

'My head is spinning from all that you've told me,' Sarah confessed.

Toby smiled.

'I'm sorry, too! I'm keen on my subject, you know. I've probably tried to explain far too much at once.'

Sarah wrinkled her brow.

'From what you say, Toby, we must pick a good name to start with. Do you have any ideas?'

'Only that it must suggest what your business is about.'

Julia leaned forward to make a suggestion.

'We could call it Gannon's, or maybe Tewit's, after the manor?'

Toby touched her hand gently and from his smile Sarah could see that Julia's preference was returned.

'Tewit's is a pretty name, but it sounds like nothing I've ever heard of. What does it mean, anyway?'

'It's a dialect name for a pewit,' Sarah told him.

Toby sat back in his chair and mused aloud.

'Birds, birdsong, eggs, nest live on the moors. Moorlands — you will be selling herbs as well as flowers. How does Moorlands sound to you both?'

'I like it!' Julia said at once, bestowing a fond smile on her beloved.

Sarah took a little longer to think it over.

'I like it as well. Moorlands sounds fresh and is more suitable for herbal concoctions. We could sell eggs perhaps and honey as well as our lotions.'

'Moorlands it is then. Hurray! Our business has a name!' Julia cheered.

Toby advised the girls to make a list of their most popular items and to work out the cost of the ingredients for each pound of soap or pint of liquid. Sarah was fascinated to see that he had a complicated mathematical formula for working out how much they should charge compared with the cost of producing them.

Sarah's head felt sore as she struggled to take in yet more new concepts.

'I do wish we'd studied economy rather than history and the harp.' She sighed. 'I feel so ignorant.'

Toby was quick to support her.

'You are both doing marvellously,' he assured her. 'To be honest, I'm surprised that a couple of women are learning so fast.'

The indignant Julia flew at him with a cushion, beating him about the head in a manner that suggested she was only partially in jest. Sarah made herself scarce. It was time to visit the duke in any case.

He was so happy to see her and

urged her to visit him so sincerely, that she was now walking up to the castle every day. He tired quickly, so she never stayed long, although it surprised her how much there was to tell him on each visit. Today he listened to every word, nodding his head.

'Toby is quite right to say you are doing well. Remember, he has had twelve years to learn his trade. You and your sister were brought up in a very different world until only a few weeks ago. Do you miss it, my dear?'

'I've been too busy to think about it!' Sarah admitted frankly. 'But now that I look back, I don't miss it. We were happy enough then, that's for sure. But perhaps it was a little dull. Life is so interesting at the moment.'

'Ah, you rise to a challenge. That's good.'

They were interrupted by the soft voice of the doctor.

'It's time for your bath, Your Grace.'

The duke smiled.

'It's such a pleasant experience now

that I have your soaps and lotion, Miss Sarah. The water smells utterly delicious and I emerge refreshed.'

The doctor nodded his agreement.

'I am glad to catch you, Miss Sarah. I was wondering if I might beg a bottle of your lotion for another patient of mine. You might remember Squire Foxton. He's completely bedridden now, poor man. His attendant is massaging him with goose grease at present, which is excellent for preventing bedsores, but his wife complains of the smell and the effect on her linen.'

'Of course I will!' Sarah exclaimed, fishing in the basket that lay under her seat. 'If you are not in actual need of a new bottle today, Your Grace, I could give this one I brought for you to the doctor.'

The duke's eyes twinkled.

'I forbid you to give that lotion to the doctor.'

Sarah put the bottle down hastily.

'You keep this one and I'll send another one to Squire Foxton's house.'

Now the duke laughed out loud, enjoying his joke.

'My dear, you misunderstand me. I forbid you to give away your lotion. Are you not in business now?'

'Why, yes,' Sarah said slowly. 'Yet how can I ask for money from our old friend, Squire Foxton? Papa has known him for ever.'

The doctor coughed. Privately, he mightily disapproved of the idea of ladies in trade, but he was devoted to the duke, and if the duke supported the idea, so did he.

'The benefits of the lotion will be such that I have no hesitation in saying the squire will find himself at no loss whatever sum he might spend on it.'

The duke smiled.

'And what sum will that be, Sarah? Has young Gregory run his mathematical formula over my lotion.'

'Indeed he has,' Sarah replied slowly. 'It will cost four pence a bottle, Doctor Gerald.'

The duke seemed to be savouring a

moment of utter enjoyment.

'My dear, dear, Miss Sarah, I do not think you need to worry about the speed of your progress within the business world. See how competently you handled your first sale!'

Unfortunately, matters did not continue to progress so well. There was no difficulty with making the herbal preparations. The sisters had been refining their recipes for years, and it was a simple matter to increase the volume of production. Toby found them a supplier of the most delightful glass pots and bottles, and helped to choose a suitable cold-pressed paper to wrap up the soaps and bath salts.

The problem of labels was solved when Mrs Grimshaw found Julia weeping over writer's cramp. It turned out that the gardener's wife could not only write, but produce the most beautiful copperplate. She insisted on coming to the house every day and writing out every single label.

'After all you've done for me, miss,

it's the least I can do.'

'The woman's a marvel,' Julia told Sarah.

'Is Grimshaw behaving any better?'

'Worse, if anything. He's refusing to have anything to do with the idea of commercial production, although in a way, things have improved. He sulks in the potting shed all day. So at least the lads can get on with their work.'

The girls sighed together over their horrible head gardener, but they were too busy to spend long on impossible problems.

'When will you make your first visit to Harrogate?' Julia asked Sarah.

It had become understood between them that Sarah should become their salesperson. Sarah took a deep breath and adopted a confident tone.

'Tomorrow.'

Julia looked at the ranks of glittering bottles, the copperplate labels, the piles of soap nestled in rustling paper.

'It'll be a huge success,' she prophesied.

But she couldn't have been more wrong . . .

8

After her sales visit to Harrogate, Sarah went to Whitewell Castle before she went home. Without her realising it, the duke had become her greatest support. He listened so carefully to every detail of the obstacles and hurdles that they all encountered. He encouraged her when her spirits failed.

The approval of such an aristocratic figure was balm when Sarah had been on the receiving end of outraged disapproval from less broad-minded members of Society. And there was another reason why she went to the castle first. She was putting off the awful task of telling her family how completely she had failed.

'I tried every shop,' she told the duke miserably now, 'every single shop. Harrogate is so vast, but I am certain that I missed not one. Toby made me a plan from a street map and I have ticked off every single establishment.'

The duke surveyed her woebegone face.

'Did any of the merchants suggest that they might be interested in your wares were they slightly different in any way? A new label perhaps or a different kind of scent?'

'I didn't even get a chance to unpack my basket, except for one place where the odious owner looked at every single item before telling me it was trash! I think he was doing it to be cruel, for the other merchants were adamant that they would not buy anything from a woman.'

'Perhaps young Gregory could act as your sales agent.'

'I could not ask it of him. In fact it's worrying me, because I know that when I tell him my sad tale, he will offer straightaway. But he's really not strong enough yet. No, I must think of something myself.'

'My dear,' he said, smiling at her with

the warm friendship that was building between them, 'I know you will find a solution, and I will wait with eager expectancy to hear about it on your next visit.'

It was all very well for the duke, Sarah mused as she dawdled home, racking her brains for an answer. All he had to do was to sit at home and wait for the next thrilling instalment. Stories of hardship were all very well, but the reality was more unpleasant than she could have dreamed.

Her whole soul burned with the complete rejection she had experienced. She had never realised how much respect she had enjoyed as Miss Sarah Gannon, a lady of quality, until she had endured the humiliation of doing without it. She tried to hide the worst of her feelings from her family, but she could tell by their responses that they had sensed what she didn't tell them. Julia made her a herbal tisane, and her papa was especially loving. He gave her a kiss on her forehead.

'Go to bed now, sweetheart, and all will look better in the morning. Maybe your old papa will think of something.'

'But I thought that you did not care for the idea of us entering trade.'

'What's done, is done, and our old life is no more. If a sapleen like young Gregory can do so well at this trade business, I see no reason why a Gannon shouldn't succeed.'

Sarah curled up in bed feeling immeasurably better. It was wonderful to see Papa feeling like his old self. Surely if Patrick Gannon were on their side, things could only get better.

He was gone at first light, to Harrogate, James said. The girls were puzzled that Papa would miss saying goodbye to Connor, but their cousin didn't seem at all surprised. There was a merry gleam in his eye as he assured them.

'We had a chat last night, Patrick and I. Don't you be fussing yourselves. All is well.'

He galloped off down the lane in a

cloud of dust, dogs and horses.

'What can Papa be doing?' Sarah asked. 'He hasn't taken the basket of samples, so how can he expect to sell any potions?'

'By buying a shop!' Patrick Gannon announced, when he finally returned home that evening.

'Papa! How?'

'Where?'

'What kind of a shop?'

'How did you pay for it?'

'Is it ready to open?'

Patrick Gannon roared to them both to be quiet! He laughed as the girls subsided. After the shame and depression of the last few weeks, it was good to see the open joy on his face.

'I knew I'd be surprising you all! Your cousin, Connor, has been good enough to lend me the money, and don't be worrying about paying it back, for it's little enough that I needed. I have purchased the sorriest-looking little wreck of a shop you were ever imagining. It'll need a great deal of work, but no matter, we'll take a few men from the manor. It is right in the middle of Harrogate, looking out over those green fields they call the Stray, and if we don't become a sensation then I'm even greener than I'm cabbage-looking.'

Julia flung her arms around her father and Sarah was right behind. It felt so good to be in harmony again, to be a family once more.

Fixing up the shop gave Sarah plenty of news to relay to the duke.

'I had no idea that shopkeeping was such an exhausting business,' he told her. 'My dear child, you always make me feel better. I am deeply indebted to you for making my last days so much lighter with your visits.'

'But I am in your debt also. You have been a good landlord and a wise adviser to me.'

The duke seemed to be wrapped in a cloud of sad thoughts.

'It's the very quality of our friendship that makes me regret my isolation here. I grew weary of the flattery of Society, and the way that every person I met seemed to want to use me for their own advantage, so I shut myself away, soured on human nature. If it were not for you, my dear, my last days would have been very tiresome. I would have had too much time to reflect on my woes, and perhaps I would not have raised the courage to put right an old wrong, but now I have done so, thanks to you.'

'To me?' Sarah said, astonished. 'You have not even mentioned any such matter to me.'

'But you set me a good example, my dear. I was weary and cynical about my fellow human beings until I witnessed your courage and determination.'

He met her gaze frankly and Sarah saw that the feeling in his blue eyes ran deep.

'Despite all the obstacles you had to climb, you never hardened your heart or threw away the love of your family as so many do when their spirits are troubled. It's often the way that we hurt those we love most.'

Sarah guessed that the duke was referring to a past mistake. She stayed silent and listening as the duke took a letter from his pocket.

'From my son,' he said softly, and there was a world of love in his voice. 'My oldest son, who has been out of my life for these ten years past.'

Sarah had always known that the young man who had the wild parties was the youngest son, but she'd never given a moment's thought to the fact that to be a younger son, one must have an elder brother.

'I shall not weary you with the whole story, but I could not seem to manage my life after my wife died. I had lost the one person who always helped me deal with myself. Anger was my only way of expression, and I vented it on my boy. We quarrelled bitterly and he's contrived to keep out of the country ever since. I knew well enough that he could manage a home leave from the army if he wished it. I had always meant to mend the quarrel when he returned, but he never did, so we remained estranged.'

'And now?' Sarah encouraged him softly.

'You made me realise that if something is important then one must be active and fight for it. I buried my pride and I wrote to my boy. The answer is here. He is coming directly.'

'I'm so glad,' Sarah murmured.

She could see that their long and emotional conversation had tired the duke, but he looked so well and so serene that she was sure a good night's sleep would restore him.

'You'll come tomorrow?' he asked her, with a trace of good-humoured mischief in his face. 'I shall be thinking of you all day. I cannot wait to hear about the grand opening!'

'Of course I'll come,' Sarah promised him. 'But it might be rather late.'

It wasn't actually dark as Sarah ran up the path to the castle the next evening. The old butler opened the door as usual, but as Sarah walked into the hall with him, she saw that he'd been crying.

'Is the duke ill?' A cold sensation gripped her heart.

'Oh, Miss Sarah, I've been in his service for forty-five years and you could never have hoped for a better master.'

Now Sarah could taste the atmosphere in the house and she didn't need the sad fact to be put into words.

'I'm very sorry to hear it, Wilson. Is there any way I can be of help?'

'No thank you, Miss Sarah.'

'Then I'll take myself out of your way.'

But before Sarah could turn around and leave, a large dark man strode impatiently into the vast hall.

'What the devil are you about, Wilson?'

'I'm sorry, Master John. I'm just coming, Master John.'

Boots clicking, the stranger strode towards them, intent on seeing what had delayed his butler. His hard gaze swept contemptuously over Sarah, her countrified muslin gown, the basket of herbs and soaps she'd brought to show the duke. He dismissed her and returned to the old butler.

'I should think so, too! Dallying in the doorway with peddlars! If you must deal with them, do it in the kitchen and in your own time. There is a great deal to be done and you must know it.'

He gave them one last, angry glare and turned away decisively. Sarah saw now that he was still wearing his uniform and his clothes bore marks of long travel. The oldest son, returned from the war! She turned to Wilson.

'Did he arrive in time?'

'The Lord be praised, Miss Sarah, he did, but I must tell Master John that he's mistaken in calling you a peddlar. His Grace, that is, as I must call him now. The old duke would be furious if he thought you were slighted.'

Sarah put a gentle hand on the arm of the distressed, old man.

'It doesn't matter at all, Wilson. He will have travelled hard in order to arrive in time to be with his father. He'll be tired. Think no more of it.'

The old butler still looked troubled, but Sarah slipped away before he could frame a response. He had enough to deal with this melancholy day, and, as she told Julia later that evening, it was of no consequence what the new Duke of Whitewell should think of her. Julia agreed.

'Wasn't the rest of the day glorious? Didn't the shop look magnificent? I can't believe how much money we made, more than a month's rent in one day. Of course, Toby says we mustn't forget our expenses, but I'm sure we're going to be all right. And, Sarah, wasn't Papa magnificent? He seemed so happy to see everyone. He was the perfect host!'

'It's so good to see him happy again,' Sarah agreed. 'In fact, he's looking better than he has since mother died, as if he's woken up, somehow. Maybe a new venture was just what he needed.'

Sarah was yawning and heavy-eyed

by the time they'd finished discussing a long list of items which needed their attention. The shop had only been open for one day, and already she could see a thousand things she'd never realised would need attention.

At breakfast the next morning, her sheet of paper was crossed and double-crossed as her list got longer and ever more complex. She spoke her thoughts aloud.

'Thank goodness for Toby and all his experience! I need to ride over this morning and consult with him. Will you come with me, Julia?'

Julia looked tempted, but she shook her head.

'I must ride over to Harrogate and help Papa, but even if I leave now, I shan't be there before eleven o'clock. Sarah, we must get an assistant. Surely it will be cheaper than Papa staying in a hotel so that he can open the shop promptly in the morning.'

Sarah made a note on her list.

'That's true, and breakfast isn't the

same without him, either!'

Julia chuckled and as she stood up, Sarah saw the butler appear.

'What is it, James?' she asked.

'Mr Mellor has called.'

'Didn't you tell him that Papa's in Harrogate?'

'He has come to see you.'

'Me? Whatever for? In any case, I don't have time today. Could you ask him to come back?'

'He made it clear that his business was of a pressing nature.'

Sarah hurried to meet the family lawyer. If life could be upset once by a terrible blow, lightning could strike twice. What if there was something wrong with the lease of the manor, or Papa didn't really own the shop? Mellor greeted her sombrely.

'Good morning, Miss Sarah. I trust you are well?'

'What's wrong? Mellor, what is it?'

'I have come to inform you that the funeral of the old Duke of Whitewell will take place on Thursday and it was

112

His Grace's wish that you should accompany the family back to the castle and be present at the reading of the will.'

'Oh!' Sarah said blankly, and then inspiration struck.

'Oh, bless him! The dear man. He kept saying that he wished me to have a pretty necklace that had belonged to his wife. I refused, of course, but he must have remembered me.'

Mellor nodded gravely.

'As the legal representative for your family, I shall accompany you.'

James showed the lawyer out, but Sarah didn't make a start on her huge list. Last night she had simply accepted the death of her old friend, but now, like a cut from a deep knife, she felt all the pain of his loss as the reality hit her hard. It was some time before she could stem her tears and turn her attention to all that had to be done.

9

Julia had expected the business to be a success from the start, but Sarah had not been so sure. The humiliating memory of the rejection her wares had received at the hands of the Harrogate merchants was vivid, and it had undermined her confidence.

She needn't have worried! The rush never stopped. The brass bell on the door of the shop tinged and pinged the whole week through as shoppers poured through the door. Taking Toby's advice, they had made the shop look pretty. The glass sparkled, the wood was polished with beeswax and lavender, and they didn't stint on candles. Moorland's Herbal Emporium was a blaze of light, and the products flew off the shelves.

Sarah soon noticed that her medicinal preparations were as much in demand as her lovely soaps and shampoos. She made a note on her ever-present list to ask Toby what he thought about hiring an assistant with some medical knowledge. In the meantime, she noted down what stocks had run low and what she needed to make the next day.

There was so much to do, that she hardly gave the old duke's will another thought until it was time for his funeral. They closed the shop out of respect and, along with many other mourners, the whole family walked through the park to the private church that was attached to the castle.

The service was beautiful though solemn. Afterwards, Sarah was glad to have Mellor's support as he guided her to a library with a breathtaking Gothic ceiling. About twenty chairs had been arranged in front of a large desk. A rank of bewigged and very important-looking lawyers sat behind the desk, and various aristocratic members of the family were taking their places in front. Sarah took a background seat and looked around.

She didn't recognise any of the family except for the younger son, who looked pale, puffy and unhealthy. Then there was a stir as the older son, the new duke, strode in. His fashionable mourning garb made him look even larger and more dangerous than his uniform had. He spotted Sarah at once, and gave her a hard look from his slate-grey eyes that suggested she had no right to be there. It upset her, and she hardly heard the reading of the main part of the will, until they came to a codicil bearing her name.

'And to my dear friend and the sweet companion of my last days, I leave the freehold of Tewit Manor, an annuity of one thousand pounds a year for life, and the topaz and diamond necklace known as the Star of Clear Sunshine, for it will suit her beauty to perfection,' the lawyer read out.

As the family dispersed, murmuring a little and casting her a few backward glances, Sarah held on to the edges of her hard, wooden seat so that she didn't fall off. When a shadow fell over her, she knew who it was before she looked up and met those scornful eyes.

'I think you should leave now, but rest assured, I will arrange to have your loot sent on to you.'

The sting in his words rendered her speechless. She got to her feet. Then she just stood there, looking up at the duke's tall body and granite face. She couldn't take a step away from him because her knees were shaking. His eyes were the coldest grey she had ever seen.

'Why do you stare at me so? If you're thinking of transferring your affection to the next duke you can forget it. I'm not in the petticoat line!'

Sarah's response came out in a soft plea.

'You are so mistaken!'

The new duke was the hardest man she'd ever met. His expression grew blacker still and his eyes were like thunderclouds as he replied.

'The language in my father's will made it perfectly clear that he was a fool about you.'

The insult to her old friend cleared her head at last. She met her accuser's eyes confidently.

'He was a gentleman, sir, and you would do well not to judge his relationships by your standards.'

And so saying, she swept out.

The episode troubled her, and although she was busy from dawn to dusk in the following days, her thoughts kept returning to the encounter.

A week later, her hands were measuring dried lime flowers into packets of tea but as usual her mind was dwelling on the painful exchange, so it was a relief when Julia came to find her.

'A letter from Grace, by special delivery, no less.'

'Surely not! Whatever could be so important?'

The letter was blotched and stained and bore all the hallmarks of haste.

Julia squinted despairingly over the scrawling and mis-spelled letters. Eventually she put it down with a sigh.

'I do not think the actual words matter. Grace is distraught, as you can see. She has been told of our venture.'

Sarah felt guilty.

'We should have told her ourselves.'

Julia nodded.

'She doesn't know about Papa's gambling, of course, and how he lost Tewit Manor. How could we have put that in a letter?'

'I'll write back,' Sarah said. 'Tomorrow, when I've got time.'

Patrick was with them for breakfast one morning a week or so later.

'This Mr Palmer seems like a steady enough fellow, to be sure,' he said for the hundredth time that morning, referring to their new assistant.

'Toby thinks very highly of him,' Julia said.

Just at that moment, James entered the room.

'Mr Mellor is here, accompanied by

legal representation from the Duke of Whitewell's estate.'

Sarah was glad of her papa's support as they joined the lawyers in the library. The gift of Tewit Manor she handled well, signing paper after paper with a hand that was quite steady. The next item, however, was different. She burst into tears when she saw the necklace. It was a fabulous, glittering treasure. Topazes worked into the shape of suns gleamed out from diamonds in the shape of not just a necklace but a deep circle of jewellery designed to cover six inches of the throat and fall in a cape on the shoulders. There were matching earrings, six heavy bracelets and a tiara. The set added up to a king's ransom in beautiful topaz, gold, and diamonds.

'I cannot possibly accept such a valuable gift! I was thinking of a locket, a token of remembrance from my dear friend.'

Unable to control her tears, she left the room, but she couldn't help hearing her papa agreeing.

'It would be unseemly in a young girl to accept it. People are talking enough as it is. Be off with you now and you can come back tomorrow to settle the rest of the business.'

Later, as Sarah was sitting with her family, she looked at Patrick, expecting him to agree with her again.

'I don't want to accept any money, either,' she told him. 'I'm happy just to have my old home back.'

But instead of agreement, she saw what looked like panic flare in her father's eyes.

'You must do as you wish, daughter,' was all he said, but as he stood up and left the room, Sarah saw that his fists were clenched.

'Julia, what's wrong?' she asked, sensing something was amiss.

She saw her sister hesitate a little, and then decide to tell the truth.

'We didn't want to worry you, Sarah, but we're sadly in debt.'

'But the shop is making so much money.'

'Yes, but we incurred a great deal

of expense in setting it up, and Tewit Manor costs a fortune to run.'

'Do we owe a great deal?'

Julia didn't answer directly, which in itself told Sarah a lot.

'You must do as you wish, but I cannot see the harm in accepting the duke's annuity.'

'You wouldn't have kept the necklace?'

Julia answered reluctantly.

'No.'

But then her expression lifted and she chuckled gaily.

'But I'd have tried it on before I gave it back!'

Sarah spent a sleepless night but in the end she decided to accept the annuity for the sake of the family.

She was glad that she had when she saw how relieved Julia and her papa were. Now that they had the worry of the bills out of the way, they could concentrate on the herbal business, which continued extraordinary well.

Another special-delivery letter came from Grace. Julia put it in the fire.

'You don't want to read it, Sarah! Our dear sister doesn't seem to have considered how she would get on without an income. You sent her more money this month, didn't you?'

'Yes, I did.'

'I'm afraid she's very angry with us for going into trade. It seems that she had been snubbed by some folk in London. I wonder if it's a man she's concerned about. I had the impression she'd met someone.'

'I wonder — ' Sarah began, but she was interrupted by James.

'His Grace the Duke of Whitewell,' he announced.

Sarah's hands flew to her hair and she was deeply thankful she was wearing her yellow muslin. Julia looked charming in blue, and Sarah felt proud of her lovely sister as she curtsied to the duke.

The impact of the man filled the tiny morning-room where they had been sitting. He was still in mourning and he wore very, very formal clothing. His broad shoulders filled out a black jacket of exquisite cut, his cravat was a marvel of spotless white folds, his waistcoat was perfection and his boots shone like glass.

Sarah waited for the man to speak. He said not a word, however, so eventually she raised her gaze to his face. She was astonished to see that he was looking uncomfortable, but his eyes met hers directly.

'I wished to see you on a matter of some delicacy.'

Julia made a motion as if she would leave, but Sarah caught her sister's arm in a tight grip. No way did she want to be alone with this man. Julia patted Sarah's arm to show that she understood before prising Sarah's fingers off her arm. Julia then went and stood by the window, looking out over the lawns. Tactful, maybe, but too far away to be of any help. Sarah had no choice but to face the duke and try to speak calmly.

'Well?' she asked.

He glanced down at his hands, before looking up.

'I owe you an apology.'

He hesitated, and despite everything, Sarah felt a glimmer of amusement. He could hardly explain what for without insulting her again!

'Let us forget the matter,' she suggested quickly.

She saw relief flare in his eyes, but he made no other comment. James now entered the room, offering refreshment in his stately manner. To Sarah's amazement, the duke accepted a drink. He continued to stand stiffly and it wasn't until the butler coughed meaningfully that Sarah realised the poor man couldn't sit down until she and Julia did.

Once seated, the duke made stiff, boring small talk while twenty slow minutes ticked past. At last, Julia gazed at the closing door as he left.

'What was all that about?' she gasped.

'I don't know,' Sarah replied, 'and I

don't know if it will make the gossip better or worse. Oh, don't look so surprised. I'm no fool, Julia, I know what people are saying of my friendship with the old duke, and his will.'

Her sister put a comforting arm about her waist.

'It'll all die down in a month, Toby says.'

But a month could be a very long time, Sarah reflected. Her feelings were already rubbed raw by the way that opening a shop had subjected them to snobbery, but at least she really had started a business. She felt sick to her stomach each time she got a hint of how her innocent relationship with the old duke had been twisted. Unreasonably, she transferred much of her anger on to his oldest son. It wasn't actually his fault his father had been a bit flowery in his will, but somehow she just knew that her life would be happier without the presence of that odious man.

They were much too busy to wonder

for long about the purpose of the duke's morning visit. The still-room was busy from morning to night and they took on another maid to do bottling. Wagons rolled up the drive bearing fruits and extra flowers. They dug up another field to add to the garden. Although it was too late in summer now to do a great deal of planting, Julia had drawn up a set of magnificent plans and was busy calculating her seed order for next year.

Patrick was a joy to be with now. The sisters realised how dull he had been since their mother died. They had got used to a father with no sparkle. Now he was full of the joy of life and it was a great pleasure to see him roll up his sleeves and tackle the business with gusto. It was a relief, too, to have his steady hand at the helm. The worst of the bills were gradually being settled, the hysterical letters from Grace finally ceased and the business glowed and prospered. In all it was a happy time.

Such times never last for long, of course!

Only a few weeks later, Sarah was busy in the shop on a mild, August day. She'd only called in to deliver her new orange soaps, but Mr Palmer, Mr Palmer's new assistant and the two boys they had hired to do the sweeping and wrapping were all busy and there were still customers waiting, so she had stayed on to help out.

Busy as she was, she gradually became aware of a dark and threatening presence in the shop. A large, pudgy man with a red face was walking slowly around the building, scowling as he examined every item and watched the flow of customers. Sarah approached him directly.

'May I help you, sir?'

He swung around as if she had offered to fight him and she recognised him now. It was the cruel merchant who had made her unpack every item in her basket before sending her away as trash. His face was red and his eyes shone with anger.

'You can help me by closing this shop down.'

Sarah was taken aback by the violence of his manner. One look at his sneering features told her that there was no chance of a friendly resolution to the encounter. His voice rose as he continued to shout.

'Women! You should stay at home where you belong. Women don't know nothing about business, and nor should they.'

Nettled, Sarah retorted.

'Well, if we know nothing about business then why are we so successful?'

She realised her mistake as soon as she saw the anger flaring in his face. Her remark had acted on his temper like throwing oil on to a bed of live coals. He clenched both massive fists. For a second she thought he would strike her, but instead he swung around and swept a dozen glass bottles of rosemary hair shampoo off the counter. The bottles hurtled to the floor. The glass splintered, green liquid gushed, and the pungent smell of rosemary filled the air.

Mr Palmer, Mr Palmer's new assistant, the two boys and three customers all turned around quickly, and then froze, staring at the breakage. Just at that moment, the brass bell of the shop pinged and the new Duke of Whitewell entered the shop. He took a quick look at the scene, then raised his voice.

'Forbes! Jones!'

Two enormous footmen entered the shop, quickly followed by a groom in blue livery. The duke looked calmly at the podgy merchant.

'I believe that you were just leaving, and that you will give me your word that you will not be returning.'

Sarah could see that a part of the angry merchant was not under control. He wanted to go on and smash up the whole shop, and for a few seconds it seemed as though he might. Then he opened his mouth and roared.

'Why? Why should I go, and leave this slut's shop open so that she can steal what's left of my business?'

The duke gestured implacably towards the door.

'I believe that a free market economy operates in Harrogate.'

The furious man glared evilly around the shop, but he left. Then the duke waved out his manservants and went over to Sarah. His grey eyes were lighter than she'd even seen then and softened by concern.

'Are you all right?'

'I must thank you.'

'And I must remonstrate with you.'

The duke cast a scornful glance at the willowy Mr Palmer.

'Why do you not have a good strong man in your shop?'

'Mr Palmer is excellent at his trade,' Sarah responded warmly. 'And how could I have dreamed that protection would be needed?'

He responded quite kindly.

'You have money on the premises and that must always be a temptation. But did you not realise that feelings were running high against you?'

'Sir, I did not.'

He frowned.

'Shopkeepers in general are not prone to direct violence. I would guess that your visitor would be alone in his direct approach, although it gives you a clue as to how the wind is blowing. No, I would suggest that you be more on your guard against sabotage, sneaking acts of vandalism and petty annoyance.'

'Oh!' Sarah cried. 'The drainpipe!'

The duke lifted one dark eyebrow and she explained hurriedly.

'One of the new pipes became detached from the wall just at the point where a flood would do maximum damage. You know how it rained on Monday night. The storeroom floor was awash by the time we opened up in the morning.'

She raised horrified eyes to meet the duke's gaze.

'But surely that was an accident. No-one would wish to cause such pointless destruction.'

The duke pointed to the mess of smashed glass on the floor.

'There are a dozen bottles you cannot sell. From some points of view, their destruction would be a good thing.'

Sarah's skin went cold all over as she realised that people in the town might wish to do her such harm. She could hear a loud buzzing in her ears.

'I must sit down.'

That evening, curled up on Julia's bed, Sarah told her sister that she was astonished how well the duke took care of her. He had shouted out immediately for Mr Palmer to fetch her some smelling salts, and rubbed her cold hands between his own warm ones until her faintness passed. He set the boys to clearing the mess, charmed the customers into promising to return and then insisted on leaving a sturdy footman on guard.

'He said we should have a night watchman,' Sarah said.

Julia brushed her tumbling locks thoughtfully.

'He could be right. Toby says the town's shopkeepers are furious about our success.'

'Why didn't you tell me?'

'Sweetheart, you've got enough to worry about, and we might have been imagining a threat. Now that we know we are not, we'll hire a man. Everything will be fine.'

'We need another assistant in the shop as well. There were people waiting to be served when I arrived today.'

'Never mind the shop! Tell me more about this duke of yours!'

'Not mine!'

'Then why is he acting so out of character? Dukes simply do not talk to shopkeepers. What did he come in for, anyway?'

'Twenty-five guineas worth of soap. It's for his London house.'

Sarah expected Julia to point out that dukes didn't usually buy soap in person either, but she was off on another train of thought.

'Toby says we should consider

opening another shop in London.'

Sarah was flabbergasted.

'What? But I'd only imagined a local business, just enough to keep us all. We couldn't manage it, anyway. We know nothing about London.'

A soft flush rose to Julia's cheeks.

'Toby would run our business. He says we could make a fortune.'

And what Toby says, goes, Sarah reflected as she kissed her sister good-night. And why not? It was clear he would be family shortly.

She tucked herself up in her own bed, meaning to think about Toby and his ambitious plans to build an empire, but instead she found herself thinking about the duke. He had been so kind today, so incredibly strong and capable, so concerned for her wellbeing. She tried to put him out of her mind but a few seconds later she was thinking about him again.

While he was abroad with his regiment, his life must have been very different from here. Over the last few months, she'd had ample proof that far lesser members of Society than a duke did not care to associate with people in trade, let alone treat them so kindly. But he would still be used to living informally with the minimum of protocol. That would account for his behaviour. Doubtless, as he got used to his new life and his new position, his behaviour would alter to suit his new circumstances, and in a very few months he, too, would not dream of visiting a shopkeeper.

Seven days, however, were obviously not enough time to alter a man's behaviour, for only a week after the encounter in the shop, Sarah looked up from her work in the lavender bushes feeling as if an alarm bell had rung. She was shocked, and yet she wasn't surprised, to see the duke pacing across the lawn towards her. She watched him get closer.

'Good morning,' she said finally, when he did not speak, merely smiled.

'I wished to thank you for returning

my footman,' he said eventually.

'He was a great help, and thank you for sending us Bailey to watch the shop.'

The duke's eyes smiled.

'I was trying to find a good situation for him. I was in Salamanca with Bailey, and he never let me down.'

Sarah glanced at the duke shyly, wondering if he missed his old life.

'You must have seen exciting times.'

She saw an angry light spring to his eyes and his lips parted as if he was about to share a recollection with her, and then steel shutters seemed to roll over his eyes and Sarah felt him close her out. They stood in silence for some time, and then she ventured to speak.

'Would you care to come into the house for some refreshment?'

'Oh, no. I do not stay. I was merely passing.'

And he turned on his heel and left her.

Sarah went back to picking the sweet lavender in the sunshine. White butterflies danced over the bushes. One stopped right in front of Sarah, flexing its lovely wings. She paused in her picking for a moment and demanded, 'What was that little visit all about?'

But the butterfly had no answer!

10

For some reason, Sarah didn't mention the duke's visit to her family, nor the fact that she very frequently looked up from her work or when driving home to see the duke passing by, although all he ever did was greet her stiffly. She didn't mention any of it at all, although she had plenty of opportunity to, for the man's name came up in conversation more than once a day over the next few months.

The old duke had kept his estates in good order, but he had been content with the old-fashioned arrangements. The new duke soon set the countryside buzzing by pulling down old cottages and ordering new ones, altering planting and sowing patterns that had stood for years, and planning to plant a bewildering variety of new crops. The county could talk of nothing else and they said that his autumn ploughing ideas were a scandal.

Rumours flew, but nobody knew exactly what happened between the older brother and the younger. All anybody knew for sure was that the wild parties stopped and so did the parade of strange visitors. When the first whispers began that the young lad was to join the army, Sarah remembered the spoiled, puffy face she had seen in the library on the day of the will reading and could hardly believe it.

The duke continued to patronise Moorlands Herbal Emporium in person. Despite their new female assistant, Sarah was still spending a lot of time in the shop, so it was incredible how she missed him every time. Not that she wanted to meet him, of course!

His visits certainly helped their position in Society. People might not approve of a duke entering a shop in person, but while he made it so clear that he cared to associate with the Gannon family and their enterprise, they were no longer snubbed so completely. They were not invited to social occasions any more, but people bowed to them if they met, and most importantly, the cream of Society shopped at their shop.

'Which is really all that matters,' Julia said, watching the regal departure of Lady Greenwood.

Sarah agreed.

'She was a little frosty, but she spent nearly thirty guineas.'

'We'll need to get more stock out this evening,' Julia said, looking at the depleted shelves.

'I'll do it,' Sarah said. 'You've been here all day and you look tired.'

Julia yawned and then looked at her sister with a laugh in her eyes.

'I cannot argue. I shan't feel bad about leaving you, with Bailey to watch over you. I'll ask Papa to meet you for the journey home at eight o'clock.'

'Make it nine,' Sarah said. 'There's a lot to do.'

They compromised on eight thirty

and by then it was time to close up the shop. Sarah locked everyone out and then made her way up the stairs to the upper floor of the building, which they had turned into a stockroom where items could be stored after leaving Tewit Manor and before they were needed in the shop.

Very shortly, she heard the shop bell jingle as Bailey arrived back from his dinner break to take up his duties as night watchman. Because of his war wound, he didn't attempt to mount the stairs but called up to Sarah.

'Everything's fine!' she called back. 'Get yourself off to bed.'

They had turned the old ground-floor stockroom, where the disastrous flood had been, into a bedroom for Bailey. As an old campaigner, he slept lightly and woke to make regular rounds during the night. Sarah blessed the duke for sending them Bailey. They had put a massive chair in the shop and Bailey spent the day there, keeping a regal eye on everyone. There hadn't been a breath of trouble since, and their losses from pilfering had dropped.

So confident in him was she, that, when she heard a knock on the door, followed by low voices and the jingling bell, she payed them no heed, but carried on sorting and counting her stock, marking which boxes she wanted the boy to put on the shelves in the morning.

Absorbed in her work, it was some time before she realised that she was smelling more than a soft autumnal flavour of smoke and burning leaves. She lifted her head and sniffed sharply.

'Bailey?' she called.

There was no reply, and now she realised that smoke as well as dusk had gathered in the corners of the upper room. She snatched up the candle and raced to the top of her stairs.

'Bailey?'

There was no reply, but her straining ears picked out a muffled sound she did not like.

'Bailey!' she shouted again, and,

picking up her skirts, she flew down the steps, two at a time.

She descended into thicker and thicker smoke. The shop door stood slightly ajar to the outside world. Inside the shop, all was silent and undisturbed, and then she saw smoke hissing out from under the door that led into Bailey's room.

Sarah felt as if her knees were giving way under her as she approached the door. Her heart was thundering so that she couldn't make out if there were other sounds behind the door or not. She coughed in the thickening smoke and flung open the door. It was a terrible mistake. Air from the shop rushed into the back room and the blaze that was smouldering there flared up. All her instincts were to slam the door and run, but where was Bailey?

Sarah felt as if she were in a dream as she took a split second to snuff her candle, a precaution which struck her as ridiculous even at the time, and dropped to her hands and knees. Deep in her brain she could hear all her instincts screaming and yammering and telling her to run as fast as she could away from the fire, but she told them to be quiet and crawled towards the blaze. She needed to know that the room was empty.

Her eyes were running from the smoke, but she could clearly see one boot stuck out stiffly from under the small, wooden cot. Her skirts got in her way and maddened her as she crawled towards the bed and then behind it. Bailey's mouth was open and his face was such a livid hue that she had to force herself to go nearer to his body and the hand she put to his neck shook violently, but there was a pulse. The man was alive!

Even down on the floor, it was so hot, and there was no time to think about what to do. Sweat ran down Sarah's nose as she pulled at the heavy man by his shoulders. If it hadn't been for all her recent labours digging in the garden and moving hundreds of bottles, she'd never have been able to move the old soldier at all. As it was, she could barely shift him.

She ended up with her back to the door she was making for, bumping along the floor on her bottom in the most ridiculous way, but it meant that she could get her hands under the old soldier's shoulders and drag him. It was so slow, though! She could see the flames growing and leaping and flickering out towards her as they grew stronger.

Her skirts ripped, and that was a relief for she could move her legs without the fabric wrapping and clinging, but as she panted and gasped for air, the smoke that ran down into her lungs threatened to smother and choke her. The heat was a torment, and it frightened her dreadfully.

She contemplated putting Bailey down and running for help, but as the roaring of the flames grew louder, she knew that she couldn't. In even a very few seconds, it was going to be too late.

Sarah's mind felt quite calm as it grew hotter and lighter and the flames burned up around her. Her body was still shuffling and dragging and coughing and panting, tugging and pulling at the heavy weight that was holding her back and allowing the flames to touch her. But her mind was astonishingly calm and she felt detached from the scene and the sights which were most probably going to be her last ones on earth.

Then she felt a heavy blow on her back and she heard an angry voice shouting in her ear. The smoke was making her stupid and she couldn't understand why the Duke of Whitewell should be beating her about the head and shoulders. He then took her arms and lifted her bodily towards the exit. She looked back and tried to protest, but all that came out of her mouth was a dry squeak.

'Bailey!'

Then she saw the duke's two large footmen rush past her. Between them, they picked up the old soldier. Sarah felt tears of relief stinging her poor red eyes and she went limp and allowed the duke to carry her out into the street.

The clear night air made her cough violently, and it was some time before she could stop. The duke kneeled next to her on the cold pavement, looking urgently into her eyes.

'Are you all right?' he demanded.

'I'm fine,' Sarah gasped, and it was true.

The damage was only to her clothes and hair. The duke's massive shoulders relaxed a little, but his eyes continued to search her face.

'Are you sure?'

Sarah shivered in the cold air, and she realised that her dress was in tatters. She was showing her legs where the skirt had ripped away.

'Your cloak!' she begged.

The duke wrapped her up quickly, and she was grateful, for the fire had attracted attention and the pavement was more thronged every minute. He looked into her eyes for a second, his expression intent.

'I'll be back. I must see about Bailey and call the fire brigade.'

Sarah nodded. Without the duke next to her, she felt like a fool sitting on the pavement, but she felt too shaky to stand up. She was happy to see the firemen arriving, although they didn't start work at once. She wanted to reassure them that Toby had insisted they pay up their insurance, but she could only manage a weak, coughing noise. Fortunately, a terracotta plaque high above the shop doorway bore witness to the fact that they were entitled to protection, and the firemen quickly spotted it and began to tackle the blaze.

The fire that had so nearly killed Sarah soon calmed down under the hands of professionals. By the time Patrick arrived, frantic with worry for his daughter, the fire was nearly over, and the building saved. Patrick went directly to Sarah. He kneeled down on the pavement and held her in his arms for a long, tight hug.

'Let me go, Papa!' she protested, finally, wincing as the words scraped her sore throat.

He let her go and stood up, mainly because the chief fireman wanted him to inspect the shop.

'The damage!' Patrick said sadly, gazing in dismay at the black and dirty hole the fire had made of the old storeroom and the chaos the smoke and the water and wet brooms of the firefighters had made of the shop.

The duke returned, and Patrick caught both his hands. His eyes glittered with the tears that spilled from them.

'But what's a bit of damage when man's greatest treasure is saved? Sir, I owe you what's dearer to me than my own life, and if it's anything you are ever wanting at any time, 'tis Patrick Gannon you must come to first. I've never been a man for the blarney, but you must know I owe you the world.'

Sarah watched the two men as she sat on the pavement, wrapped in the duke's coat. It was darker and colder now. Many of the passersby had moved on, but a good number hung around, talking over the excitement. Wet, acrid smoke curled and licked around the scene. Sarah felt as if she'd never get the smell out of her nose and her lungs.

Looking down, she saw that her hands were dirty and shaking. She wished that her papa would come back and hug her again. She had a childish wish to be picked up and comforted, and her whole soul longed for a hot bath and a cup of tea. But the duke was still in earnest conversation with Papa, and to her utmost astonishment she heard his words.

'There is, as it happens, sir, a very great boon you may grant me.'

'Name it!' Patrick shouted, slapping the duke on his shoulder. 'You've only to name it and it's yours! Whatever I have is yours for the taking!'

'Then I would beg that you would do

me the honour, the very great honour, of bestowing your daughter's hand upon me in marriage.'

Sarah tried to get to her feet but her knees were too weak to support her and the effort set off another coughing fit. She sank back into the folds of the duke's cloak and coughed and coughed into the warm folds of wool. What on earth were the two saying? She struggled as hard as she could to subdue her poor lungs, and eventually emerged into the night air again, eyes streaming, to hear Patrick speak decisively.

' 'Tis a great honour you do me, to be sure, Your Grace, and you have my leave to go courting to your heart's desire. But it's not for me to be saying whom my girls should marry. You may not approve but it was settled between my good wife and myself that the girls should have their free choice in the matter.'

Sarah looked at the duke, furious with him. She was filthy, she was upset, she was sitting on a pavement in the dark and all she wanted him to do was go away and leave her alone. Instead, he left her father and came swiftly to her side. He kneeled before her so that his eyes were level with hers. His passion was overwhelming. Urgency seemed to drive him forward.

'Marry me, Sarah!' he said.

His eyes shone, and his words came out with such fervour that they sounded like a command. Sarah forgot that she owed this man her life and only remembered how dreadful she was feeling.

'Go away and leave me alone!'

He was surprised and his eyes showed it.

'Do you not wish to marry me?'

Sarah's words came from the depths of her exhausted and overwhelmed being.

'I want to go home and I shall never leave it. Tewit Manor is where I belong.'

The duke continued to kneel for a few seconds longer, looking at Sarah with dark shadows in his eyes. She couldn't tell if he was sad or angry as he questioned her softly.

'Sarah?'

She turned her head away in a gesture that was to haunt her for months.

'Papa! Take me home!'

Patrick approached a few steps and then stopped, looking at the duke and hovering uncertainly. The duke got to his feet and strode away. Sarah watched his coatless figure receding, and she burst into tears. Patrick took the final few steps towards her, kneeled down and took her in his arms.

'Shush now, my darling. Papa will take you home.'

11

Home, however, seemed to have lost its charms. Sarah decided that she must have a much weaker constitution than she had ever suspected. One tiny fire had undone her completely.

Patrick, worried by her pallor and listlessness, sent for the family doctor, who agreed that the fire was to blame.

'Such an event causes a trauma to the nerves and the muscles of the whole body. Miss Sarah must rest and recuperate until the damage to the system is repaired.'

But the more Sarah rested, the worse she felt, so she decided to get up and go back to work in her stillroom. She didn't care to visit Harrogate or the shop, although she listened when Julia told her of all the renovations and improvements that were getting underway.

She soon heard that the duke had left for London. She and Patrick had agreed to keep the duke's proposal a secret, and so far as she knew, not another soul knew of it, which was a relief. Her papa obviously wanted to talk about it, but Sarah snubbed him firmly every time. She had said no, the duke was gone and the whole matter was closed.

Oh, but life was so weary! Sarah wondered if she was going into a decline. Why else would she feel so despondent? She wasn't eating, she wasn't sleeping and she couldn't summon up a speck of interest in life. Even the news that Julia and Toby were to marry at Christmas failed to lift her heart, although she was careful to feign every happiness.

As the days turned into weary weeks, she went about her work with her face set in a cheerful mask, and to her utter surprise, her family was fooled. It hurt a little that they should not notice her true feelings, but they were all so busy.

It was agreed that Toby should open a new shop in York and another in Leeds before tackling London. He and Patrick went on a trip to find premises and interview possible shop managers. They also took on more staff at Tewit Manor, gardeners, mainly, but also staff to help with preparing and packaging the herbal lotions. Patrick took especial care over the gardeners. He confronted Grimshaw and informed him bluntly that a new gardener was to be in charge of the commercial production.

'How did Grimshaw take it?' Sarah forced herself to ask.

Julia's blue eyes were merry.

'He has a new job! A consortium of Harrogate merchants is going to make herbal preparations. They believe that our head gardener is responsible for our success, so they have offered him a great deal of money to leave us, and I'm delighted to say that he's going to leave his wife as well, just while he gets settled, he says, but I don't think he'll be back. Never, in my wildest dreams, could I have imagined such a satisfactory ending to the story of Grimshaw.'

Sarah turned away, not caring. What did it matter? What did any of it matter? The whole household was busy and productive from morning to night and the rest of the family were as merry as larks, but she felt as if she were inside one of the big, glass jars they used to protect early plants — cut off from the world and even her own feelings.

It was all down to the shock her nerves had sustained in the fire. The short, November days were made even shorter by constant cloud and heavy rain and Sarah dragged her weary body and despondent mind through the daily routine, trying to look normal while inside, she wanted to crawl into a deep, dark hole and stay there for ever.

Sarah was feeling the most depressed she'd ever been when a letter came from Grace. Julia came running to find her.

'We haven't heard for such ages. Let's have tea in the library.'

Julia seemed not to notice Sarah's heavy spirits. She shook out the letter and read about three words before shrieking in surprise.

'She's getting married! Our Grace is getting married!'

Sarah couldn't work up any interest, but she asked dutifully, 'Whom is she marrying?'

Julia looked up from the letter, her eyes full of shock.

'The Marquis of Blackburn!'

'She can't!' Sarah exclaimed.

Julia had never looked so troubled.

'Did you tell her about the gambling?'

Sarah tried to remember exactly what she'd put in her letter. It hadn't been easy to write, and perhaps she had erred on the side of discretion.

'Sort of.'

Julia's brow furrowed and she spoke slowly, thinking matters through.

'In all fairness, the man cannot be blamed for playing cards with Papa. It was Aunt Octavia who was at fault.'

She looked at Sarah frankly.

'I do not understand how it has come about that Grace is to marry the marquis. Aunt Octavia told us that she was his special friend, and see, Grace tells us to write to her at Lady Violet's which suggests that she's now there.'

Then she sighed.

'Grace has gone so far away from us now that I do not see we have any say in the matter. There was a letter for Papa which I can now guess is the marquis asking his permission, but even that will only be a formality. There is nothing we can do to sway Grace's decision.'

Sarah felt sick to her stomach, but she had to act.

'We must. I must go to London and see her. If Grace knew his true character, she wouldn't wish to marry that man.'

Julia surveyed Sarah's face while her quick wits added up facts and came to a conclusion.

'You never told me much about meeting the marquis at The Swan, only that he had passed on the deeds. Did something happen?'

'He is a monster, and I cannot let Grace marry him. He would make her unhappy.'

'When Toby and Papa get back from York, we'll ask Papa to go.'

Despite the unpleasant nature of the task that lay before her, Sarah felt more alive than she had for a month.

'We can't wait for them, and besides, Papa doesn't know what I do. I shall go myself. Shall I take Rose or Emily?'

Sarah was halfway to London before it occurred to her that she didn't know with whom she was going to stay. Aunt Octavia was out of the question. She could hardly turn up at the Duchess of Kent's and announce that she was Grace's friend and did they have a spare room she could stay at, and she barely knew Mother's relations at all.

At least her dilemma helped to distract her from the way the stagecoach rumbled and jolted over the appalling roads. She spent the rest of the journey making a mental list of relatives and deciding in which order to approach them. As it happened, her list was unnecessary. The very first person she tried was not only home but delighted to see her and completely unfazed by the unconventional way Sarah had turned up without warning.

'Darling girl, how lovely to see you! You've just missed Connor, but he gave us such a good account of you all and now that I have you in front of me, I can see that it's true. Dear Sarah, you're blooming.'

Aunt Kathleen was famous for her Irish nonsense, but her warm welcome and gentle flattery was balm to Sarah's troubled soul. She gazed into her aunt's merry eyes and blessed the good humour she saw there.

'Aunt Kathleen, I'm so gad to see you. I was afraid you'd be at the castle,' she confessed.

'In this dreary murk?' Her aunt shuddered. 'The men might like to be out in the dark and the wet, killing wee furry things, but a sensible woman goes shopping in this weather. There's a lovely play on at the theatre tonight. Shall I see if I can get you a seat now?'

'Thank you, but I'd like to see Grace this evening if I possibly can.'

Her aunt gave her a warm kiss on the cheek.

'Of course you would, darling. I was forgetting that your own big sister was here in the town. It's very grand she's becoming. I hear she's to marry the Marquis of Blackburn.'

Sarah suppressed an urge to ask Aunt Kathleen what she knew about the man. Her aunt seemed to have no strong feelings about the marriage one way or the other.

'Is the engagement generally known?' she asked.

'No announcement has been made, if that's what you're meaning, but you'd know that, being her sister. No, it's more that they've been an item for a wee while now, and the marquis has told more than one person that he's found a soul mate in Grace.'

'She cannot know what he is,' Sarah said to herself sadly.

She continued to feel miserable as she unpacked. Her news would destroy her sister's happiness, but she could not keep her secret and let her sister find out about her husband's true nature after it was too late and they were married. Grace was doomed to misery at some point in the affair, that was for certain. It was better to enlighten her now. She would be devastated, but she was still young. It was better that she should find out now, while there was a chance she would recover and perhaps one day make a truly happy marriage.

Aunt Kathleen lent Sarah a maid, for Rose was completely exhausted by the rigours of the journey and the excitement of being in London. The footman showed them the way to Cavendish Square, where the Duchess of Kent had a large house. Grace wasn't exactly thrilled to see her little sister. There was nothing but petulance in her dark eyes.

'I'm going out in an hour. You should have sent word that you were coming and I would have called.'

'I must see you,' Sarah told her.

'Funny Sarah, do you have to be so intense? You can come and keep me company while I dress.'

Grace's bedroom blazed with candles and not one but two French maids were in attendance.

'Run and ask Lady Violet if I should wear the pink masquerade dress or the orange,' Grace instructed the maids, and then she turned to her sister. 'We are to go to a masked ball at the Duke of Clarence's this evening and there are to be fireworks over the river.'

In answer to a shout from outside, the second maid left the room and Sarah's heart beat fast. She seized her sister's hands.

'Grace, I must talk to you quickly while we are alone. Dearest, I have news that will be very painful. It's about your betrothed.'

'Tarquin?' Grace questioned carelessly. 'He has no secrets from me. If you mean to upset me with news of his ladybird then you are mistaken. I know all about her and I approve. She's not nearly as pretty as I am and she caters for certain tastes that I don't need to worry.'

Grace snatched away her hands and fished in a tiny gold box for a beauty patch. Sarah's whole world rocked, but she pushed aside the implications of her sister's last comment. She couldn't take the time to think about them now. She was too keyed up to carry out her mission.

'Grace, listen!' she commanded urgently. 'I tried to write to you about Papa's gambling, but perhaps I didn't make it clear.'

Grace swung away from the mirror and glared at Sarah.

'Clear enough! And if you think I shouldn't marry Tarquin just because he won at cards you're an even bigger fool than I already think you are. At

166

least he knows how to hold his drink and when to stop gambling, unlike that silly old fool who calls himself our father. He's the one you should be warning me about. He nearly ruined my life! Lucky for me that Tarquin likes shocking people! Do you know what my chances of good marriage with anyone else are now that you're in trade? None, that's what! Tarquin is my only chance, and I'll never give him up, never!'

Sarah met the hostility in her sister's eyes with shock and disbelief. It was as if she were looking at a stranger, not a child she'd grown up with. She knew now that she'd failed in her mission, but Sarah was no quitter and she was determined to have her say.

'There is more, dearest, I only tell you this because I'm afraid that he'll make you unhappy. I'm afraid that the marquis is not always honourable.'

Sarah was struggling for the words to describe the horrible episode in The Swan. Grace interrupted her with a short, hard laugh.

'You mean that he would have seduced you and then not lived up to his side of the bargain? I laugh every time I think of your face if you'd discovered that he no longer had the deeds.'

Both maids ran back into the room, screeching about hair and being late. Grace turned back to the mirror. Her eyes met her sister's in the mirror as she spoke first to the maids and then to her sister.

'Give me the pink dress and I'm ready, Really, Sarah, you are being very tiresome. Go back to the country and leave me in peace.'

Sarah was shaking all over. She knew what she'd heard but she did not believe it. She knew in her heart that Grace was lost to her, yet she could not quite bring herself to give up the fight so easily. She snatched up the discarded orange cloak and mask and donned them.

'I shall come with you.'

'Go away!' Grace hissed angrily.

A slim, laughing figure in a purple dress ran into the room — Lady Violet.

'Grace, you are ready? Why, whoever is this in the orange?'

'My pesky little sister!' Grace snapped. 'And she is not coming with us! Take that dress off Sarah. It's mine and you shan't have it.'

Sarah saw Lady Violet's thoughtful green eyes studying her over the top of her purple mask.

'Let her come with us, Grace. You will spend all evening with your lover and that's very boring for me. Come on. The carriage is waiting.'

Lady Violet's cape whirled as she spun around and ran lightly down the stairs. Sarah followed the two cloaked figures down the grand staircase and into a splendid carriage.

Sarah knew that Grace was correct and she'd wasted her time in accompanying her. She wished with all her heart that she'd stayed at home.

The party was splendid and although Sarah did not know it, it was much tamer than usual. Masked balls were often used as a way of letting off steam, but the Duke of Clarence was a stately old fellow and so the revellers kept well within the bounds of propriety.

A tall figure in black and white attire very soon claimed Grace, and Sarah made no attempt to stop him. She could see Grace's pink mask nodding and glittering as she chatted, and she felt sick when she thought of the two of them discussing her. No doubt they would find much to laugh at in her attempts to stop the marriage.

Sarah stood back against a wall out of the way of the whirling, glamorous throng of dancers. Her head ached and she wished with all her heart that she was at home. She stood there for some time until a long, commanding drum roll drew her attention. A master of ceremonies stepped to the front of the long ballroom.

'My lords, ladies and gentlemen, before the unmasking at midnight, it is my very great pleasure to announce a betrothal. The gentleman in the black and white domino is to marry the lady in the pink domino, and as they take to the floor, I'll leave you to see if you can guess their identity before the clock strikes.'

The orchestra played a slow, romantic tune and the figure in black and white bowed to the pink lady with a flourish of his cape. As the two figures took to the floor, bending and swaying in time to the music, Sarah was hardly surprised at all to see that her sister had no qualms about dancing a waltz in public. She could hear murmurs behind her as people tried to guess who the mystery pair was. It didn't take the crowd long.

'Blackburn!' a decisive male voice said behind Sarah. 'He's been taken up with that grocer's daughter for months.'

A man agreed.

'I wish them the joy of one another. Blackburn's a queer fish, and the trade connection is not one I'd care to make myself.'

As similar whispers filled the air around them, Sarah's heart burned. Then there was a stir in one corner of the room. A tall, masked figure in a black and red cape was shouting.

'It's a lie! It's a lie, I tell you!'

The couple danced on, oblivious, but more and more heads turned as the person in the black and red ran out on to the dance floor, shrieking, 'He's mine, I tell you. He's to marry me!'

There was no mistaking the harsh, loud tones. Aunt Octavia! Now Sarah saw a bare arm holding a flashing silver blade appear from the silken folds of the black and red cloak. The couple danced on. Sarah's heart pounded. Surely there could be no real danger.

Nobody in the ballroom seemed to think so, for none of them moved, simply watched in fascination as the black and red domino continued to shriek. As her passion rose, the words became undistinguishable. Then the two dancers became aware of the shouting black and red figure.

First, the pink domino and then the black and white domino broke step, and as they faltered to a halt, so did the orchestra. The room fell silent, save for the cries of the demented, knife-wielding, figure.

'Mine! Mine! Mine!'

The Marquis of Blackburn took off his black mask and surveyed the statuesque, wailing figure before him. His eyes glittered as if he were enjoying himself.

'You are even madder than you look if you thought that you had any chance with me.'

He laughed softly as Octavia lifted the knife again.

'She stole you! If it wasn't for Grace, you'd have married me!'

The marquis turned away with a shrug that was an insult. Sarah was gripped by a premonition that sent her running across the polished floor, at the same time as the grotesque figure of her aunt let out a final scream.

'She shan't have you!'

Aunt Octavia lifted the silver knife high in the air and then plunged it down towards the very centre of the folds of the pink domino, aiming for Grace's heart. The crowd around the centre of the dance floor gave a great collective gasp and their clothes rustled as they all moved a little closer to watch, but none of them went to Grace's aid.

The marquis turned back to watch what was happening, but he made no move towards the demented woman. There was only Sarah. Her whole being was focussed on the path of the knife as it flashed through the air. Afterwards, she could never understand how she moved so quickly. One moment, she seemed to be three feet away, watching the sharp blade slice towards her sister, the next moment she had hurled her whole body at her aunt and she was hanging on to the arm that held the weapon.

The blow was deflected to one side, ripping harmlessly through folds of pink silk. Sarah could hear Grace screaming, but the silly girl still didn't move away, and the marquis made no attempt to come to her aid. Aunt Octavia shook off Sarah, and she lifted the knife again. Sarah moved towards her, but she knew that alone, she wasn't strong enough.

'Help me stop her!' she screamed.

Finally, a large figure in a forest-green outfit came to her aid. As the cape swirled, Sarah caught a glimpse of iron-hard muscle. For a moment there was a confusion of yards of coloured silk, and then the knife went spinning harmlessly across the polished dance floor. The figure in the black and red domino was lying on the floor, raving and screaming in a sound that was at once dreadful and pitiful, and Sarah was staring into the grey eyes behind the forest-green mask, and all her depression was gone for ever.

12

You!' she said softly, as the Duke of Whitewell took off his green mask and threw it to the floor, giving Sarah one swift look, before he turned his gaze to the mad woman on the floor.

'She needs attention,' he commanded.

'Grace might know who her doctor is. Do you, Grace?' Sarah asked, but the figure in the pink domino was crying, sobbing hysterically.

'I don't know and I don't care! She nearly killed me! She should be locked up.'

Now that the danger was over, the crowd pressed close, all chattering excitedly and looking at Octavia's writhing form with avid eyes. Four burly footmen came panting on to the scene. The Marquis of Blackburn marched over to them.

'Where were you when there was

trouble? Your master shall hear of this!'
he shouted, then he took Grace's arm
and led her away.

The footmen looked at Octavia a
little doubtfully. Raving lunatic or not,
she was a lady of quality and they were
not quite sure how to proceed. One of
them looked at Sarah.

'What shall we do?'

'Take her back to her home in the
first instance. I shall come with you.'

Sarah became aware that the duke
was still by her side. His grey eyes were
so loving that she felt as if the sun had
come out.

'You'll care for her, even after the
injury she did you?'

'She's family.'

'I'll come with you, if you'll allow it.'

The warmth of his support was
better than a warm blanket on a cold
night. Sarah smiled up at him happily,
not bothering to disguise her pleasure.

'Thank you.'

As the duke read her happy expression, his own brightened with delight.

He said no more to her directly, not while they supervised the removal of Aunt Octavia from the ballroom. Sarah suspected that, by herself, it would have taken her a great deal longer to persuade two of the footmen to accompany them in order to hold down the raving woman and to send one of the other footmen to extricate Aunt Octavia's carriage from the hundreds that lay waiting for the ball to be over. The last one was sent to persuade a reluctant doctor to leave his card game and attend her poor aunt, but with the duke by her side all took place with a magical simplicity.

The doctor administered a drug which subdued poor Aunt Octavia. They all stood watching as it took effect. She subsided into an uneasy unconsciousness and the footmen were able to let her go. Even in her sleep, she was twitching and mumbling and the doctor shook his head.

'You should put her in an asylum tonight.'

Sarah's heart was distraught.

'Is there no hope?'

The doctor hesitated.

'It's unlikely that she'll recover her senses, but I do know of a private hospital where she can receive the latest treatment, if you wish to try that.'

'Of course I do.'

The doctor and the footmen took Aunt Octavia away. Once at her home, Sarah gave her aunt's staff a few simple instructions and promised to return the next day.

Despite the winter's cold, it was a relief to walk out of Octavia's sad house and into the fresh night air. The duke's carriage was waiting outside. Sarah was about to decline, but then she saw that Rose was there, ready to accompany her. She looked up at the duke and smiled.

'Thank you for fetching my maid.'

His eyes flashed as he looked back at her, and there was no mistaking the meaning in his tone.

'There could be no greater happiness

than in thinking of your pleasure.'

Sarah stepped into the carriage and allowed herself to be wrapped in a thick blanket. There was a hot brick for her feet as well. As she sank into the warmth and the comfort, she realised how tired she was. The duke sat opposite her, smiling gently, and this time she was able to smile back, confident that he'd trouble her with no wild declarations of love while her head ached so badly.

When they reached Aunt Kathleen's, he jumped down and handed her out of the carriage himself. At the open door of the house, he kept her hand in his for a split second longer than necessary. Sarah looked up at his strong-featured face and no longer found it hard or harsh. His eyes were soft with his feelings for her.

'There is something that I very much wish to ask you. Would you allow me to call on you tomorrow?' he whispered to her.

Sarah smiled mischievously.

'Why wait until tomorrow? Later today will be perfect.'

He smiled at her then and happiness flashed in his eyes before he turned away.

Sarah felt a smile curving her lips as she made her way into the house and to bed. She slept deeply and well, and was already awake when Rose brought her a tray at lunchtime. The little maid's eyes were as round as brown pennies and her hands were shaking as she laid down the tray, but she never said a word.

'Rose,' Sarah questioned, 'this silence isn't like you.'

'If you please, Miss Sarah, your Aunt Kathleen said that she'd scalp me if I let out so much as a peep and as soon as I've woken you I'm to run back down and help with the drawing-room. She's got every man jack in the house scrubbing it out to be gorgeous for the duke's proposal.'

There wasn't a soul to be seen when Sarah made her way down to her aunt's best drawing-room later that afternoon, but she saw with a deep sense of pleasure that the room looked beautiful indeed. All was polished and glowing and radiating a deep, peaceful harmony that seemed in tune with the way she felt herself. A little winter sunshine shone through the sparkling windows, and it seemed as if the universe was arranging itself for the benefit of her very special happiness.

The duke was announced only a few minutes after she entered the room. He stood by the door, as if he was afraid to walk in. Sarah enjoyed the moment and his tall, handsome figure for a few seconds longer and then she looked at him and smiled.

'You came.'

He crossed the room swiftly and there was all the love in the world blazing from his eyes.

'Nothing could have stopped me. Dear, dear Sarah, will you marry me?'

She met his loving gaze and was supremely happy.

'Yes,' she answered simply, 'but I'm afraid that Grace means to marry the Marquis of Blackburn.'

The duke smiled at her.

'We shall see him only as often as you choose.'

'And I do not think that Papa will give us his business. He's enjoying it too much.'

'I shall be his greatest customer.'

'And Julia is to marry Toby Gregory, and he is planning a whole empire of shops.'

The duke caught her hands.

'Dear, darling Sarah, there is nothing that would prevent me from marrying you. I am yours. I love you as I never knew it was possible to love a woman, unreservedly, with all my heart, for ever.'

Sarah felt ecstasy flashing through her heart as she registered his sincerity. He took her hands and drew him down next to her on to the brocaded sofa. Her heart bounded with both fear and deep pleasure at his proximity.

'You're not afraid of me?' he asked her gently.

Sarah met the intensity of his gaze.

'Only a little, and not of you, of your feelings, perhaps.'

He bent his head and kissed her hands. His touch was both calming and exciting and Sarah looked at his bent head and the vigorous black hair that curled over his collar and stretched out a daring hand to touch the soft dark strands.

It was the most intimate moment of her life.

He lifted his head again and met her eyes, smiling.

'Dear Sarah, I frightened you by being so impetuous after the fire.'

She couldn't help smiling.

'We were on a public pavement, and I was all dirty, with holes in my dress!'

It seemed as though the duke found it funny now as well, for he threw back his head and laughed.

'I couldn't have chosen a worse moment to declare my passion. Dear

Sarah, do you forgive?'

She looked down at their lovingly-entwined fingers.

'It seems that I have.'

Then she looked up and couldn't resist teasing him.

'But I thought you weren't in the petticoat line.'

He groaned.

'What must I do to atone for my past stupidity? Forgive me, my darling, I believe that I loved you even then, for the very idea of you belonging to another man had me in a jealous rage. I was stupid, but you must allow that I constantly endeavoured to tell you so.'

'Once, that's all,' Sarah told him.

He kissed her hands again and then her cheek. When Sarah dropped her gaze in shy confusion he kissed the top of her eyelids in a manner that was utterly delightful.

'Only once did I get the words out, but did you not wonder why our paths crossed so often? I was trying to find the courage to speak to you and explain how mistaken I'd been.'

Sarah was filled with the delightful wickedness that comes from having such a man in one's power.

'I'm surprised that you'd take such trouble over a poor peddlar girl. Most people would order them away from the front of the house and into the kitchen door.'

He groaned and laughed at the same time, but she could see genuine contrition in his eyes, which was followed by dancing laughter.

'I could remind you that a certain young lady said she preferred her own home to mine! Will you miss Tewit Manor dreadfully?'

'No, not now. A house is only bricks and mortar. It's love that makes it a home. After the fire, I was miserable the whole time.'

'Because of me?'

Sarah felt shy, but she nodded.

'Because you were not there.'

'Because I chose my moment so badly! I will spend the rest of my life making it up to you. What should I do? Shall I buy you Harrogate? Shall we travel the world? Name your pleasure and I will provide it.'

Sarah's heart swelled with the purest, most complete happiness that she had ever known. She touched his hands gently and dared to initiate a gentle kiss on his cheek.

'Only love me,' she said softly, 'and all will be well.'

The duke recognised her change in tone and he, too, became serious. His eyes were so tender and his arms so strong as he whispered to her softly.

'If our happiness is to be measured by the amount that I love you then all indeed shall be well.'

And as his lips touched hers in a loving kiss, she knew that she'd found her real home at last.

The End

We do hope that you have enjoyed reading this large print book.

Did you know that all of our titles are available for purchase?

We publish a wide range of high quality large print books including:
Romances, Mysteries, Classics
General Fiction
Non Fiction and Westerns

Special interest titles available in large print are:
The Little Oxford Dictionary
Music Book, Song Book
Hymn Book, Service Book

Also available from us courtesy of Oxford University Press:
Young Readers' Dictionary
(large print edition)
Young Readers' Thesaurus
(large print edition)

For further information or a free brochure, please contact us at:
Ulverscroft Large Print Books Ltd.,
The Green, Bradgate Road, Anstey,
Leicester, LE7 7FU, England.
Tel: (00 44) **0116 236 4325**
Fax: (00 44) **0116 234 0205**

Other titles in the
Linford Romance Library:

TO CAPTURE A HEART

Karen Abbott

When Gill Madison visited the beautiful Malaysian island, Langkawi, at the end of a backpacking holiday, she knew she would love to spend more time there. Being on the spot for an offer of a 'Girl Friday' job on board a pleasure boat seems to good an offer to turn down, especially when the skipper is as handsome as Bart Lawson. However, Gill soon discovers that it isn't all to be plain sailing.

FATEFUL DECEPTION

Kate Allan

When Captain Robert Monceaux, of the Fifteenth Light Dragoons, rescues Miss Lucinda Handscombe from a highway robbery, she piques his interest. Robert cannot stay away from her, and Lucinda becomes attracted to him. When her guardian demands that she accompanies him to Madeira against her will, Robert offers to save her. But, after a misunderstanding, Lucinda runs away. And when Robert eventually finds her, they realise they must learn to trust each other for their future happiness together.

GROWING DREAMS

Chrissie Loveday

After the death of her long-absent ex-husband, Samantha Rayner and her young daughter Allie move to Pengelly in Cornwall to start afresh. When they stumble across the overgrown grounds of Pengelly Hall, Sam starts dreaming of restoring them to their former glory. Jackson Clark, the business-minded owner of Pengelly Hall, agrees to fund the project, but could Sam have taken on more than she bargained for . . . And what secrets does head gardener Will Heston hold in his past?

MAIL ORDER BRIDE

Catriona McCuaig

Lydia McFarlane has been used to a life of wealth and privilege, but when her father remarries, her new stepmother starts a systematic campaign to remove Lydia from the family home in Ontario, plotting to marry her off to a man who doesn't love her. Lydia decides to take matters into her own hands, and runs away to the prairie town of Alberta to become a mail order bride — but life in the Golden West is not as idyllic as Lydia has imagined . . .

SILVERSTRAND

Diney Delancey

Working for the Distress Call Agency, Tara Dereham travels from London to the seaside town of Silverstrand, to help Mrs Ward run her guest-house. But when Mrs Ward falls ill, Tara has to manage the business and care for her client's grandson, helped by one of the guests, Steven Harris. But there is a secret in the Ward family, and danger looms for Tara as she learns more of the secret and of the people concerned.

FOREVER AUTUMN

Christina Jones

After a heartbreaking deception, Stephanie Gibson decides to change her life completely. She moves to the south coast to work as a nanny for the large and scatty Matthews family. Her employers are friendly and eccentric, and Stephanie soon settles in. She is enchanted by her charge, Nikki, and loves the challenge of her new job. However, when she finds herself falling in love again, spectres from the past loom up. Has Stephanie made another mistake and will she ever learn to trust again?